Mind Flow Publishing & Production LLC
Presents

THE MARY B CHRONICLES
The Long Way Around

Book II

Dakiara

Copyright © 2018 by DaKiara

All rights reserved. This book or any portion thereof may not be reproduced or used in any manner whatsoever without the express written permission of the publisher except for the use of brief quotations in a book review or scholarly journal.

First Printing: 2018

ISBN

978-1-7322433-4-7 Paperback

978-1-7322433-5-4 EBook

Additional copies of this book and others are available by mail or by visiting the website listed below. Check website for pricing.

Mind Flow Publishing & Production LLC

PO Box 48768 Cumberland, North Carolina 28331-8768

www.mindflowpublishingproduction.com

Cover Design by Miss Web Designer, LLC

Dedicated To My Angels

Daquan, Deja, Dante, Kevonn and Kiara

RIP

Daquan Jamique 95 & Kiara Denise 00

Special Thanks

To GOD for Giving Me The Strength and The Words To Do This Project. Blessed by The Experiences to Draw From It Has Not Always Been Easy.

Dedicated to Some Who Have Gone Before Me

Mary Merriman

Naomi Thompson

A Glimpse into the Author

DaKiara was born in Richmond, Virginia but grew up in rural Laurinburg, North Carolina. She was raised by her mom Dorothy Merriman McNeill, along with other influences from the church community. Carlette is the youngest of three children. She has two older brothers Lee and Lamont. When her mother remarried (Chauncey), she gained three sisters and another brother (Kim, Cierra, and Ernest, Chaunnie).

She is a wife and mother to three children and two angels DaQuan and Kiara. Her writing journey began early in life around age twelve, to escape and convey her feelings and those of others around her that couldn't find a voice of their own. Throughout the years, she has used her writings to express her love, and her pain of losing two of her children, the state of the world, and just about life in general. For years, her writings were her therapy, and now, she is using it in hopes to inspire or motivate others. With her children Jacqueline, D'ante, and Kevonn all in college, and she returning two years ago, she has decided to follow her passion. With the help of her husband of twenty-one years Kenny and a host of family and friends, ninety-two strong, she is breathing life into her heart's labor.

Her writings have expanded from just poetry to now include short stories as well. Her hopes are that people will feel they are not alone in their day-to-day experiences. This is Carlette's reintroduction to the world and DaKiara's introduction. She is excited to take you on her journey. Stay tuned, the best is yet to come.

Contents

Prologue 1

Chapter 1 6

Chapter 2 17

Chapter 3 30

Chapter 4 40

Chapter 5 52

Chapter 6 63

Chapter 7 72

Chapter 8 85

Chapter 9 95

Chapter 10 102

Don't forget to sign up for 108

Prologue

Davina had always been a hustler by nature. When she was young, her mom Clarice, was addicted to drugs and worked the streets. They lived well because of her mom's chosen lifestyle. Her dad, she never knew. She had only seen pictures of him. From what her mom had told her when she wasn't high, he stayed in and out of trouble but promised time and again that he would do right by her. Bobby pimped Clarice, or Reese as he liked to call her. That was how they first got together. Davina had seen the pictures of her mom while she was pregnant, and he was with her holding her like he cared. The back of the photos simply said, 'Reese and Bobby V.'

After seeing the life her mother had—all the clothes, the money, and the men—Davina swore she would have those things too. Davina promised herself it wouldn't be the way that her mom had gotten them. Her mom was into the life so heavily that she sometimes didn't know whether she was coming or going. Before Davina became a teenager, her mother succumbed to the lifestyle. One night, she was working the streets, and a John attacked her. He thought she was someone else, and he left her for dead.

By the time she was found, she had lost so much blood, the doctors knew she wouldn't last. One doctor knew Reese all too well; he was one of her Johns. He tried his best to save her, but the guy had stabbed her too many times. Her lungs were punctured, and she was bleeding internally. All hope was lost. She died within the hour, before the cops could bring Vina to be with her. The doctor, Joshua, had met Davina and had offered to take her in so she wouldn't have to go into foster care.

Vina had remembered Uncle Joshua, as her mom called him, because he was the only one who came to the house to see her. He always brought gifts and took her to her favorite restaurants. Vina always thought Uncle Joshua was very handsome, and she loved that he would bring her gifts too. When the cops brought Davina to the hospital, he tried to explain what happened to her mom. Davina couldn't believe she was gone. She asked to see her, and Joshua didn't think it was best, but Davina was just as stubborn as her mom, so she insisted.

"I need to see her… I have to see her. Please…"

Joshua went in with her; he had instructed the nurse to make sure she was covered. That was no way for Davina to see her for the last time.

Davina broke down, and that was the last time she thought of her mom. Joshua took care of the cremation. That was the beginning of the end of Davina's childhood.

Joshua convinced Davina that it was for the best that she move into his place. She remembered the way he had treated her mom, always with kindness, so she agreed. Joshua hadn't thought twice about offering her a home. He was unable to have any children, so Davina reaped that benefit. Joshua adopted her by her fourteenth birthday.

Davina tried to make sure that Joshua was always proud of her. Joshua always treated her with kindness and showed her the finer things in life. He told her that there wasn't anything she couldn't do if she always did her best.

Lesson learned. She always did her best. She went on to graduate from high school at the top of her class. Joshua wanted her to pursue a career in the medical field, but she had other thoughts. Since she was younger, and she saw all the nice clothing her mom had, she tried to recreate some of them. She came up with a few nice outfits that she sold to her friends in high school to make extra money, not that she needed it. Joshua made sure she never wanted for anything.

The one thing she had yet to find was love. During the summer after her graduation, she met Robert. She was attracted to him because he was handsome, and he made her laugh. The one thing he was lacking was money. He was different from the other guys she had dated. She saw sincerity in his eyes.

Davina, following in her mom's footsteps, never thought she would ever be content with one man in her life. She surprised herself. She and Robert had been together for a year, and things were going well. Then, it happened. She literally ran into Christian.

He was stopped at a traffic light, and she wasn't paying attention. She slammed into his car. The damage was minimal, and, as payment, he asked her out on a date. Davina thought it couldn't do any harm, so she agreed. Robert had begun working at the local glass factory, and she had time on her hands. She was feeling a bit neglected, so she spent more and more time with Christian.

Vina liked that he took her to the expensive restaurants and treated her like a queen. She had fallen in love with Robert, but she felt like something was missing. Christian filled the void with ease. He pushed her to go for her goals of wanting to work in the clothing business. He even put her in contact with some of the local vendors he knew from school. With Christian being older than she, he was more mature, and he showed her a whole different world. He reminded her of how Joshua treated her and her mom.

Although she loved spending time with him, she realized it wasn't love. What she had with Robert was real love, and she made up her mind to stop seeing Christian. Robert had been so busy working overtime and trying to follow up on some leads with his sister that he hadn't noticed Davina had been stepping out.

Once he had saved up enough money, he asked her if she would move in with him. She agreed, and she wanted to come clean with Robert, but she never got the chance. Robert's sister had been found, and he was going through so much with her that she couldn't bring herself to give him more to worry about. He had been really worried about his sister, and he never stopped looking for her. Knowing that he loved her that much only made Davina realize he was the one for her.

Davina hadn't seen Christian in months. He had left town to do some guest speaking. That gave Davina a way to create the much-needed space from him. One night while Robert was at Mary B.'s, she reached out to Christian. She knew it was stupid, but she missed him and his touch. He was just getting back into town, so he was happy to meet up with her.

They made love one last time, and Davina told him it was over. Christian told her he would always be there for her, no matter what. And that was the end of Christian, or so she thought.

The next night, Robert came home, and he needed Davina so much. His sister was going through a rough time. This was the first time she had seen such pain in his eyes. They made love like it was their first time. For Davina, it was the first time with no thoughts of another man clouding her mind. She vowed to be faithful to him and make up for lost time.

And she stayed true to her word.

Chapter 1

Now Christian was back and not for her, but for answers. Davina had worked too hard to keep her relationship with Robert safe and secure. There wasn't anything she wouldn't do to keep it that way.

She hatched a plan to get Christian off her back once and for all. She decided to call in a favor from a classmate. Yvette was a nurse at the hospital, and she owed Davina big time. Davina wanted her to fake a paternity test once she got the sample from Christian; she needed Yvette to make sure the results didn't match up.

"Girl, you do know I can lose my job behind this."

"Come on, Vette. I really need this. You do this, and I won't ask for anything again. I promise. This is life and death for me."

"Who will the sample be coming from? The potential baby daddy." She smiled but Davina didn't find that amusing.

"Christian. Yes, the doctor on staff here, and yes, I need you to keep it on the hush."

"You are really trying to get me fired. I got you this time, Vina, but no more, not anything like this. I can't risk it. I've got kids."

"I'm sorry to put them at risk, but I need this favor. I will let you know when the sample comes through. It should be soon. Thank you, Yvette. You are a life saver."

As luck would have it, Yvette never got the chance to make good on that favor. If it wasn't for bad luck, Davina would have no luck at all.

Jean had been concerned about Robert since she had told him about her pregnancy. She didn't like the look she saw in his eyes. Although she had seen him several times since, he never shared with her about what was going on with him. She didn't want to pry, but she didn't want her brother to go down the same road she had. It wasn't pretty, and she knew in her heart that he wasn't strong enough for that. It nearly took her life more than once, and she still fought the demons.

"God, you have saved me more than I deserve, so I ask you not for me, but for my brother Robert. Keep him protected and whatever demons he is fighting, be his shield and sword."

Jean thought maybe she would ask Davina if she had noticed anything different with him. Davina said she hadn't seen anything. Jean thought that very strange. How could she live with someone and not see those signs. She understood how her parents hadn't noticed; she had stayed out of sight when she was high. Jean didn't think he was on the same drugs she had been on, but she knew it was something. He seemed super alert but then he would seem exhausted. She watched him for a while, the pattern would repeat. Jean thought for sure he was using some sort of uppers.

One day, she pulled him to the side while at Mary B's house and asked him to go for a walk. Robert seemed glad to get out of the house. She had found out where his spot was, so they went walking. She was trying to see if he would react or stop even.

"Hold up, Jean. That's one of my partners from work. I'm going to holler at him for a moment. Be right back."

True to his word, he came back, and he told the truth. What started out as a quick fix, turned into a full-blown addiction.

"Robert, talk to me. Tell me what's going on, man. If no one else sees it, I see the difference. You could never hide anything from me. And that's not going to change now."

"What are you talking about, Jeannie? I'm good, baby girl. Matter of fact, I couldn't be better."

"Robert, I told you most of what I went through. I can't watch you go through it. I refuse. So, talk to me. I'm begging you."

"Look, Jeannie, I take a little something-something to help me get through the day. You know, to take the edge off. My dude from work turned me on to it. It's harmless, man." He smiled, trying to play it off.

"No drug is harmless. That's just a lie you're telling yourself to make it okay. Does Davina know about this?"

"No, and you're not going to tell her… it's nothing to tell. Look, they changed how we make bonus at work, we're on production now. I have to keep up, to make the money needed to take care of my home. Davina's been on some other stuff lately, all secretive and stuff. This also keeps my mind right. It's simple. I'm good, I promise."

"Robert, nothing good is going to come of this. Keep your mind right… You're more messed up than even you realize. Is it something we need to talk about? Do I need to talk to Davina about something? What can I do to get you back right, bro?"

"Jeannie, I'm good, okay? I will cut back, okay? Okay?"

Jean just shook her head. She only could imagine she would have been just as stubborn, back when she was doing her thing. That's what scared her the most. She had to put a stop to it if he didn't. She would give him a little time to see if he could get it under control. She felt she owed him that much. When all else failed, she turned to God. "How can I help him?"

Two weeks later, at the glass plant, they had a random drug testing. Guess who was one of the persons chosen? Robert couldn't believe his misfortune, but they gave him a break. He had to stop using, of course, and go to a substance abuse class for a minimum of six months. He would be on leave from work, and he would have to work the program. Robert couldn't tell Davina this; she was already stressing him about money. He was so reluctant to talk to Jean, but it was her or Mary B. Jean was the lesser of the two. Jean smiled to herself, because she knew God worked in mysterious ways. He constantly proved it. Jeannie told Robert she had some money saved, and she would help him for the next few months. He also needed to get a part-time gig, and she would help keep it hush so Vina wouldn't be tripping.

"What about Tim? Is he going to be okay with you helping me out? I don't want to cause no issues in your house because of my stupidity. You tried to tell me, and I just didn't want to hear it. I guess I had to go the long way around just to get here."

"Tim loves me, this I know without a doubt. I will tell him what's going on, and he will be fine with it. He knows how important my family is to me and how important it is that you don't end up where I was. We're good. You just do what you need to do and get it together. If you work the program like it's supposed to, you should be done in a few months and then you can go back to work, and all is good."

"Jeannie, thank you. You tried to tell me. I'm sorry I didn't listen." The two of them grew even closer after this moment. Mary B. noticed the changes, the before and after. You see, Mary B had been around for a long time, and there wasn't much that got by her these days. She missed a lot with her daughter, so she promised she wouldn't do that again with them or the grands. She was proud of the fact that her daughter was there to handle the situation. She had come along way.

"William, we done all right. Our children are going to be all right." William just nodded and smiled and held his wife close. Always a man of few words until needed.

Davina was happy that it seemed that Robert was distracted, so that meant he wasn't worried about what she was up to. She was free to roam around and try to figure out how to get this thing with Christian taken care of. She had finally gotten Yvette to agree to help her, so she was just waiting for Christian to return. Davina was sure he wouldn't let it rest. It seemed like since she saw Christian for the first time at the hospital, she had begun questioning if it was possible. She kept telling herself the answer was no. There was an old saying "Tell God your plans and watch him laugh."

One day, Mary B had the grands over while the adults all went out together. William loved those children just as much as Mary B. There wasn't much the children couldn't get away with. Bedwetting was one of those things. William had noticed that the last few times they had stayed over, Kaloni had some wetting episodes. Of course, he mentioned it to Mary B in private, not wanting to embarrass his little princess. Mary B in turn mentioned it to Robert and Davina and encouraged them to get her checked out just to make sure nothing was wrong. Something seemed to be a little off with Kaloni. She was a little smaller than Kevin. She didn't seem to advance as well as he had, but that was what happened sometimes with twins, so the doctors weren't too concerned.

The next day, Robert and Davina decided to go ahead and take the children for a checkup. Davina thought she could possibly get Yvette to go ahead and swab the baby's cheeks and hold onto that until Christian came back. The twins' normal doctor sent them to the hospital to get some testing done. They wanted them to check the twins' kidneys and livers just to make sure everything was working properly. While checking Kevin's kidneys, they noticed a little scarring. As a precaution, the doctor requested they do a vision and hearing test. Just as he thought, there was a slight bit of hearing loss. Davina thought Kevin just liked ignoring them or was always pretending. After running other tests on Kaloni and Kevin, it was time to talk to Robert and Davina.

Dr. Johnson told them that Kaloni was developing a little slow, but she wasn't in any danger. They did want to monitor her kidneys to make sure they didn't overlook anything.

"My concern is with your son. He has some issues with his kidneys. There is some scarring and that concerns me. Let me ask you, do either of you have any kind of kidney diseases?" Davina and Robert both shook their heads no. Dr. Johnson looked confused. "One of you has to have some sort of kidney disease. You see the issue with Kevin is hereditary. I'd like to get you both tested as soon as possible. Eventually, Kevin may need a kidney, so we need to go ahead and test you for that too. Do you have any questions as of now? I know that I'm throwing a lot at you at one time, but it's very important that we hop on this immediately. We have some time and may be able to correct the issues with his hearing."

"Is he going to be okay? How does this happen?"

"Unfortunately, this is again hereditary and sometimes, you may not know you are a carrier or at risk until it happens. I can guarantee you I will do all I can to make sure he is okay."

"What do we need to do to get tested? How soon can we get tested?"

"We'll go ahead and take care of that today if that's okay? The twins, I would like them both to stay a few days, until we are sure about what we're dealing with."

It never crossed Davina's mind that she should call Christian. Why should it? She was sure he wasn't the father of her twins. At that moment, Davina's phone vibrated. It was none other than Christian. How does he do that?

He had texted saying he needed to see her so they could go ahead and proceed once and for all. Davina told him that right now was absolutely not the right time. Sensing the urgency in her text, he asked where she was. Reluctantly, she told him they were at the hospital.

"Call me," Christian asked of her.

"Christian, what is it? Now is not a good time."

"Vina, what's wrong? I know you well enough to know when something is not right."

"Chris, there's something going on with my babies. Robert and I are about to get tested in a few. I don't have time or the strength to deal with you right now."

"I'm on my way, Davina. I will stay out of the way, but I will be close in case you need me. I told you I'm not trying to cause problems, but I deserve to know the truth as do you."

"Please, no. Don't come up here. Not now." Christian had already hung up the phone. Shaking her head, Davina began to cry. Why is this happening now?

After taking the test, Davina and Robert sat in the office with Dr. Johnson. This time was no different from a few hours ago. He told them something they didn't want to hear, but this time it was worse. In a matter of hours, Davina's world crashed. Not only were her children having complications, the man she swore was their father only fathered one. What in the world?

"Listen, I'm sure this isn't the conversation either of you thought we would be having. Trust me, neither did I. Nonetheless, it's obvious something went on that shouldn't have. Not judging but we must think of the babies. Robert, you are Kaloni's father, however, you are not Kevin's." Robert looked puzzled. "Let me explain the best way I can. Davina, I'm sorry. Would you like to explain or shall I?" Davina just shook her head no, as the tears fell. "Robert, at some point probably within a day or two, you slept with your wife as well as someone else. Your sperm resulted in Kaloni, and the other donor is Kevin's father. I trust you know who that is, Davina? It's more important now than ever, because you both were tested for kidney disease, and it didn't come from you."

This whole time Robert sat in disbelief. He had been busting his butt to provide for this woman he swore before God and his family that he would love for all time. Only to now find out that it was all a lie. At this moment, he hated her but loved her at the same time. So much was going through his head, he was afraid to speak in fear of snapping. Davina grabbed his hand.

"Baby, you okay?" If looks could kill, Davina would have keeled over right then and there. Dr. Johnson kept talking.

"I need you to find the father, because again, we may need to get some blood, or possibly a kidney from him later. Can you do that?" Davina pulled out her phone, dialing Christian's number, "We're on the fourth floor with Dr. Johnson." Robert became sick to his stomach, and he got up to leave.

"I need some air. I'll be back." As he was walking out the door, Christian was on the other side walking in. Robert did a double take. He had seen this guy so much in the last year or so. What he didn't know was they shared a woman. Christian walked into the room, looking at his colleague, shocked that he was the father.

Chapter 2

"Christian, are you being serious right now?" Dr. Johnson asked him. "What were you thinking? Didn't you know she was involved with someone? This type of stuff doesn't happen often but leave it to you to be the one to make it happen."

"John, tell me what's going on with the babies?"

"First things first, you're the father of one of the twins. Yeah, that part. Congratulations, you're the father of Kevin. Now, onto serious matters, do you have any kidney problems? The little boy has some issues. Currently, there's some scarring on his kidneys, and this is hereditary. When he gets a little older, he may need a transplant if this isn't brought under control. We will need to get you tested just to verify that you are in fact the father."

Davina, who had been sitting there the whole time in silence, looked at Christian and then to the doctor who was looking at her.

"Yes, he is the father! I need to go find Robert. Is there anything else you need from me right now, Doctor?"

"No, not now. I personally think you have a lot of mending to do. I wish you luck with that. As for the babies, we're going to do everything we possibly can to ensure they are okay. If I don't see you tonight, I will definitely see you tomorrow."

"Vina, do you need me to come with you to talk to him?"

Davina looked horrified. "No, are you crazy? This man I love may never speak to me again." John almost felt sorry for Christian, almost, Christian often made bad choices and unfortunately, this one was the worst one yet.

When Robert left the room to get air, he just started walking once he left the hospital. He was still in shock. How could she do this to him, to them? Those babies were his life. Yeah, he had slipped up with the drugs, and yeah, he let the children get out the door, but there was nothing he wouldn't do for them. He vowed to protect them always. How could he do that if Kevin wasn't even his? His son was sick, and he couldn't do anything to protect him. Robert walked and walked; he looked around and didn't recognize his surroundings at first. As he began to focus, he realized that he had walked all the way to his spot. What was he doing here? Nothing good would come of this. He began battling the demon inside of him, but he wasn't strong enough to resist.

This time he got something different. He walked all the way home, to prepare his purchase. Robert took his belt off, and he tied off his arm. It wasn't too long until the darkness closed in around him. Robert had purchased heroin this time. The dosage that he took was enough to kill him. All he wanted to do at that moment was escape this world. As he struggled to breathe, he swore he heard Jean calling his name. The last image he saw was that of his sister.

When Davina finally left the hospital, she looked outside and didn't see Robert. She called Jean and asked if she had seen him. Davina didn't want to go through the whole story right now. She wasn't up for that task, and she knew Jean would be livid with her. Jean said she would go out looking for him. Luckily, she arrived at Robert's when she did. Calling 911, Jean checked for a pulse.

"Please, I need some help now for my brother. He's not breathing."

"Ma'am, can you tell us what happened?"

"I will tell you whatever you want to know, but I need someone here now." She gave them the address and just sat the phone down. She could hear the operator calling out to her, but she was only concerned for her brother. She began doing CPR on him. Luckily, she had been studying to become a nurse and the CNA training had helped. She never imagined she would have to do this on her brother. Her heart was in her stomach. "Robert, come on. I need you to breathe." Jean was getting frustrated, and just as she was about to give up, he struggled to breathe.

Just then, the paramedics came in and took over. At that moment, Davina also arrived home. The sight before her horrified her. This was all her fault. All she had to do was be honest and trust in the love that she and Robert had.

"Oh my God, what happened, Jean?"

"He overdosed." Within moments, the paramedics had him loaded up on the stretcher and out the door. Davina rode with him to the hospital. Jean stopped by Mary B's to pick her and William up. Tim stayed home with the children.

Upon their arrival to the hospital, Davina went into the emergency room to wait for Robert to be brought in. Davina thought the night couldn't possibly get any worse. That was until she saw Christian was the doctor on call that night. Christian immediately saw her and asked her what was wrong, and why was she in the emergency room. Christian grabbed her arm, but she jerked it away, as Jean and Mary B walked in. William was parking the car.

Jean's mind went all over the place after seeing that scene. Mary B hadn't seen it, so she was unaware.

"Hey, Christian." Davina's eyes opened wide. "Is something wrong here, Davina? Do you know Christian?"

"Jean, hey, good to see you," Christian said. Mary B walked over and asked Christian if he was related to Tim, because they looked so much alike. Davina shook her head in disbelief. She had never noticed it before, but Mary B was right. They did look alike. She took in a deep breath as they rolled Robert in.

Davina rushed to the door.

"Ma'am, you can't go in there."

"They just took my husband back there. I need to make sure he is okay."

"Ma'am, you have to take a seat. They will call for you when they're ready for you to come back."

"Are you serious right now? You're telling me I can't go with my husband?"

"I'm sorry, ma'am. I'm sure they will call you in a few."

Taking another deep breath, Davina turned around only to face Jean, Mary B, and the always quiet William.

Jean pulled no punches and she started in first on Davina. "So, sis, tell me what's going on with Robert. Then I need to know what's going on between you and Christian?" Mary B didn't realize that Tim was Christian's son, other than her assumptions when she just saw him.

"Jean, it is such a long story, and I don't want to get into it right now please. I just want to make sure Robert is okay. My babies are already here, and now my husband too. Can I get a pass for a few until I know he is okay?"

"Davina, you got your pass, but you know how I feel about my brother. But you got your pass for now." Davina's heart slowed down to its normal pace. She knew she didn't want problems with Jean right now.

Mary B and William had gone to sit down and talk amongst themselves. "William, I'm a little confused. There are so many secrets and nothing good comes of secrets." Mary B knew that all too well. William put his arm around his wife and held her close to reassure her. Jean walks over toward them, shaking her head. "What's wrong, child? Is that Tim's father?"

Jean nodded her head. "Tim wants nothing to do with him. To respect him, I've honored his wishes. I only just met him when I had the twins. He was here that night working. He is a doctor on staff. He left Tim, his brother, and his mom when they were younger. Tim said he had another family."

"That's horrible. He looked like a nice man. Looks can be deceiving. Devils come in all forms."

"That's just it, Mom. I know he has made mistakes from what Tim has said, but I know he was trying to get to know Tim. It was Tim who refused to allow it."

"I'm sure he has his reasons, child. You continue respecting his wishes."

"Yes, ma'am. There seems to be some sort of connection between Vina and Tim's dad. I wonder if she is part of the other family he has. Wouldn't that be crazy if she was Tim's sister?" Jean had no idea just how far off she was from the truth.

The nurse motioned for Davina to come back. They had managed to get Robert stable. They had to start an IV, with some medication to block the body from continually absorbing the drug into his system called Narcan. He was awake, and his breathing was being monitored. When he saw Davina, his heartbeat raced, and he became irritated. The nurse told her to please leave the room. Once he was calmed down, the nurse told him his parents and sister were also outside. Robert shook his head no, he didn't want to see anyone.

The nurse went to tell the family that he wished for no company at this time. Looking at their faces as she approached them, she wasn't happy to relay the message. She noticed that he and his sister looked a lot alike, and she seemed concerned. Concerned enough to go off on whoever crossed her. The wife was looking like she was just out of it.

The worrisome look in the parents' eyes was enough to make her own eyes water.

"Hi, I'm Bianca, Robert's nurse. Right now, he isn't up for visitors. While his wife was just in there, he became agitated and that's not good considering his condition. I know this isn't want you wanted to hear at this moment. We do have him stable, and we are doing everything we can to ensure he stays that way. So please give him a little time. The doctor does have an order for a psychiatrist to see him in the next day or so. Do any of you know what happened? What triggered this or is this something he does often?"

"No, it's not something he does on a regular basis," Jean spoke up. As she did, she cut her eyes toward Davina. "Mom and Dad, since he is stable, why don't the two of you take my car and go home. I will call Tim later to come to get me. I want to stay here; he's going to want to see me."

"Please call us the moment he is in the clear and feels like seeing us. Please make sure he knows we're here," Mary B had turned her attention to Bianca at that time. "Davina, are you going to be okay or do you want to go home for a bit? I know the twins are here. Maybe you should go home and get a little rest." Davina wasn't about to leave Jean up there with Robert. She wasn't ready for the conversation, but she didn't want her to hear it from Robert.

Reluctantly, Mary B and William left the hospital to go home. They stopped by Jean's first to see the children.

Tim asked, "What's going on with Robert? Is he okay?" \

"We're praying that he will be. We're unsure of what happened. All we know right now is that he overdosed on heroin." Tim's face turned pale as could be.

"Are you sure?"

"Yeah, son, that's what the doctor said. The nurse said he is stable but didn't want to see anyone. Jean and Davina are there with him, well, in the waiting room."

Tim's mind started racing. How could he have overdosed if he was getting help? He was close to finishing his program, and he had progressed well. What could have happened to make him get back to this place, and to touch heroin. Jean must be livid. Tim asked Mary B if it was okay that the children stay the night, so he could head to the hospital shortly. Of course, Mary B and William said it was okay.

Jean walked away and decided to call Tim; she was tired of just sitting there. The more she sat there the more she became angry, and looking at Davina didn't help. She felt like she had something to do with it. She had so many things running through her head. Jean thought maybe if she talked it over with Tim, that would help her to figure it out since.

"Hey, baby. I'm so confused right now. Did Mom come by there?"

"Yeah, they just left with the children. What's going on, babe?"

"That's just it, baby. I don't know. All I know is that this mess isn't adding up. Robert wouldn't have backtracked like that. I know he was upset about the children being hospitalized, but that wasn't something to freak out about."

"And he's not talking at all?" Jean could only shake her head.

"Do you know why your dad would be talking to Davina? I walked in on them having a heated discussion. I told Davina I would drop it for now, until Robert is better, but something doesn't feel right."

Tim looked perplexed; he prayed his dad wasn't up to his old ways again. He had been thinking about giving him a chance to know his grandchildren. Tim was thankful he hadn't taken that risk yet. Picking up his phone, he called Christian. After several rings, the call went unanswered.

Jean decided to head up to the floor where her niece and nephew were. She hadn't seen them since they had been admitted. She felt awful that she didn't know all of what was even going on with them.

Everything happened so fast. Her mind was spinning. If she hadn't worked so hard to get clean, she would have been tempted to indulge herself. But she remembered Shirley telling her to get herself together, and she knew she couldn't give in. She had often wondered what happened to Shirley. To satisfy her curiosity, about a week ago, she had called to the facility and asked to speak to her. The crazy thing was they told her there was no Shirley on staff and hadn't been in well over six years. Jean knew she had her own angel looking over her. To make sure she wasn't crazy, she checked the newspaper archives and confirmed a Shirley Mae Frazier had survived a house fire that had taken the lives of her three children. All she could do was smile at herself. Even now, Shirley was still looking out for her.

When Jean arrived at the pediatric floor, she saw Christian. At that moment, he rushed by her as they had just called his name over the intercom. Jean wondered what in the world was going on. Timing wasn't on their side. Eventually, she would figure it out or get it out of one of them. She asked the nurse who was working with Kevin, if he and Kaloni were okay. The nurse looked at her strangely at first.

Jean noticed the look and said, "Don't you remember me? Those are my twin brothers' twins." The nurse seemed to have remembered, smiled, and nodded her head yes. When Mia and Joseph were born, not long after Kevin and Kaloni, to siblings who were also twins, that was the talk of the ward for a bit. "The babies will be okay... Kevin is going to have a bit of a struggle since he has kidney disease. The odds are good that he'll be okay. I think they have a potential donor should the need arise." Jean shook her head and told the nurse thank you, and that she would be back later.

Meanwhile, Bianca had gone back in with Robert and told him that his sister and wife were both still there. She also told him that his mom and dad had agreed to leave but wanted to make sure he was okay. Robert looked away. Bianca asked if he felt any pain. Robert shook his head no. She asked if he was hungry. Again, he shook his head no. Bianca told him, that the longer it took him to eat, the longer he would need the IV to keep him hydrated. Robert took a deep breath and exhaled. Bianca asked him if he wanted her to leave. He hunched his shoulders. He didn't want to tell her to go, because he did want to talk but he just didn't know who to talk to. He didn't want to look like a fool in front of his family. He felt like garbage because he had no idea that his son wasn't his. How could he be so stupid and not know. How could he have loved this woman and she have betrayed him. His mind went back to when the doctor asked if she knew how to contact the father, and she pulled the phone out and speed dialed him like it was nothing. His whole world crashed in an instant.

Bianca could see that he was thinking about something but didn't want to push. She told him she would be back to check in on him soon.

As she was leaving, she heard him say, "I know you think I'm a horrible person, trying to kill myself and then not wanting my family here."

Bianca turned around and simply said, "I'm sure you thought there was a good reason to try to end your life. Obviously, there's no lack of those who care about you." She eased out the door. Robert felt like crap, but he didn't want his family to be the worse for it. He tried to rest his mind and calm his thoughts. He then closed his eyes so he could rest. He knew eventually he would have to face his parents, Jean, and Davina too. He just wasn't sure he was ready to do that.

Chapter 3

Davina went upstairs to see the babies. As luck would have it, she was going up as Jean was coming down, so she dodged that bullet yet again. While she spent time with the twins, Christian popped in.

"What are you doing here, Christian?"

"I'm here because he's my son. Remember, we finally established that. I told you I wasn't trying to disrupt your world. I asked you some time ago to find out the truth. This could have been handled another way if you had. Robert wouldn't have had to know. Is he okay by the way?"

"I guess. He won't see me. His sister is here, and she isn't going to handle this well either. My life is so messed up right now."

Christian looked at her and with little compassion said, "Davina, this is bigger than you right now. You had the chance to make it better, you chose not to. The only thing that matters is those children. I will do whatever is necessary to ensure Kevin is okay."

"You're right, Chris. You've always been good to me. I should have told you I was with Robert when you and I met. I thought it would be a harmless, fun thing between us. I appreciate everything you're trying to do. And I'm sorry it came to this, but with my life, I'm about my survival."

"I can dig that, so understand I'm about his survival. I truly hope your relationship can be repaired with Robert; even you deserve happiness, Davina. That's all I've ever wanted for you."

Christian walked away and didn't look back. This only proved to make Davina feel worse. She knew Robert would never forgive her, and she didn't think she could forgive herself. Only time would tell. She did know she had to be truthful and whatever happened, was what she deserved. Christian was right, it was no longer about her, and it was all about the children. She prayed Robert could at least get past what happened and still be there for Kaloni at least. Her child didn't deserve to lose her father because of choices she had made.

***

Jean saw Bianca and asked her how Robert was doing, since he still hadn't wanted to talk. Bianca told her, "He seems to be carrying a huge load. He hasn't said much to me, although I was trying to get him to talk. Robert wanted me to know that basically he isn't a junkie, which I never thought he was. He needs to talk to somebody and soon. He was very adamant about it not being his wife."

"Can I try to see if he will let me in the room? If he resists, I promise I will leave. I just need to know my little brother is okay." Bianca nodded her head as she turned away.

When Jean entered the room, Robert's back was turned to her, so she tiptoed in. She thought that once she was in, he wouldn't protest too much. She walked around to the other side of the bed and smiled when she heard him snore. Jean watched him sleeping for a while until she too dozed off. When Robert woke up, he in turn watched her while she slept. This was something they did as children and it carried over into adulthood. Jean was right. Once Robert saw his sister, he didn't have the heart to turn her away. It had been easy to send Davina away. He knew when Jean woke up, she would want answers. Robert felt like she deserved to know the truth, and he just hoped she understood why he couldn't deal with Davina right now. He decided to turn over and try to get a little more sleep before he had to deal with his sister.

Tim continued calling his dad, as he was really concerned. Jean also seemed upset by this whole ordeal. Tim decided to head to the hospital. He was almost certain that Christian was probably there somewhere. Just as he thought, he heard his dad's name as soon as he walked through the doors. He figured he would give it some time and have him paged. While he waited for him, he decided to check on his niece and nephew before going to find Jean. Plus, he wanted to talk to his dad first. That way once Jean asked him questions, he had the answers. As he got to the pediatric ward, he bumped into his father.

"Hey, umm, did you see that I had been calling you? I called about ten times or so."

"Hey, Tim. Actually, no. I hadn't checked my phone. I've been busy on the floor. There were a couple of bad accidents, and it's had me busy. What's up?"

"Jean said she saw you and Davina having a heated conversation yesterday. What was that about? For once, I need you to be honest with me."

"Tim, can we step inside the lounge, so we can have a little privacy? I've always been honest with you, even when you didn't think so. There's so much I should tell you, but now is not the time or place. As far as what Vina and I were discussing Tim, that's between us. I'm sorry but I think you need to hear it from her. I hope you understand, son."

"The one time I need you to be transparent with me, you refuse. To think, I was contemplating allowing you to be a part of my children's lives. My wife was almost begging me to forgive you."

Christian, feeling as if he was betraying his son, broke down and told Tim what was going on. "You're going to wish I didn't tell you this, but to make a long story short, Davina and I had a fling. It was just fun. I care about her, of course, but it was never serious. Before you start, no, I didn't know that she was with Robert or anyone for that matter. I asked on several occasions. It wasn't until I saw you and your wife here that first time, I saw her as well. I've been begging her for some time to get a DNA test done. You know, just to be sure. I prayed that the children weren't mine."

"OMG! So, Kevin and Kaloni are your kids? What have you done?"

"It just gets crazier, Tim. Only Kevin is mine. Kaloni is Robert's child."

Tim couldn't believe his ears. "What! How is that even possible? No freaking wonder Robert reacted the way he did. That's enough to break any man. He's been devoted to that woman since I've known him. Why didn't you come to me when you realized there was even a remote possibility you were the father? Maybe this could have played out differently. Now, so many people are going to be hurt, including my wife."

"Tim, I'm sorry. I wish this was handled so differently. I promise I tried to resolve it. I did. You must believe me. I never wanted anyone to be hurt."

Tim could only shake his head. He was partly disgusted with his father, but for some reason, he believed that he didn't know about Robert. He even believed he had tried to reach out to Davina.

"Tim, that little boy out there has kidney disease, and that he inherited from me. You may want to get Joseph screened or just keep an eye out for any signs. I'm so sorry that this is where we are, and that this has dysfunction all over it."

"I need to find my wife and make sure she's okay."

***

When Robert woke up, Jean looked him dead in his face. She rubbed his head, whispering that it's going to be okay.

"Hey, Jeannie. I'm okay. Can we just leave it at that?" Robert saw the look on Jean's face, and he knew she wouldn't drop it. He took a deep breath and started with the sordid tale. "Jean, I've been stupid. I loved Davina, even now I still love her, but I hate her at the same time. She lied to me, to everyone. There wasn't anything I wouldn't do for her, for those kids."

"I know, Robert. I know what you've been through to make sure she was happy. What concerns me is that I need to make sure you're happy. Davina will get what's coming to her."

"Jean, promise me you won't do anything stupid. She is after all the mother of my child, my children. Is it wrong of me or stupid of me to still feel as if Kevin is mine too?"

"No, bro, that just means you have a soul. Where we go from here is all on you. Do know that I'm going to kick your butt for taking some heroin. What were you thinking?"

Robert somehow thought he would get a pass on that one, but he should have known better. "Jeannie, I didn't mean to. I just wanted to forget for a while. You don't know how bad she hurt me. And then she calls him like it's nothing, and he's there in a flash. I couldn't believe it."

Just then, Tim knocked on the door. Jean nodded for him to come in. "What's up, Robert? How are you feeling?"

"Could be better, but thanks to my sister, I'm alive. I forgot to tell you thank you, by the way." Tim looked at Jean and could see the hurt in her eyes. He hated that more than anything. He still had to deal a blow he didn't want to, but he knew he couldn't keep it from her or Robert.

"Listen, babe. I found out why Davina was talking to Christian." The look on Robert's face was of disgust. "Robert, this is hard for me to say but my father is Kevin's father." Robert took a deep breath and told Tim he thought the guy looked familiar. He hadn't realized it until that moment that he favored Tim. "He didn't know you two were together, and it was just a harmless fling. He hadn't thought any more about her until he ran into her when Jean was here when she had passed out with the twins."

"This chick has been acting funny since around that time, but I thought it was just me. I just worked harder to provide for her. I nearly killed myself trying to work the extra hours and all of that. For what?"

Jean had left the room, and the guys hadn't even noticed until the door slammed. Tim flew out after her, but it was too late.

By the time he reached her, she had already connected her fist to Davina's face. Davina hit the floor hard, but that didn't stop Jean. She jumped on her and just pounded. Davina fought back, but she was no match for Jean. All the hatred and anger that Jean had held for so long was unleashed on Davina. Tim finally removed Jean from Davina and took her out of the hospital.

At that moment, a security guard walked up, asking if everything was all right. Davina, catching her breath, said she was fine. Through it all, she knew better than to make trouble for Jean. Davina gathered herself and ran for the door. An ambulance pulled up as she ran out, and there was no time for the driver to stop. In that moment, her life flashed before her eyes as the ambulance made contact. Thank God, he wasn't going fast, but fast enough that she broke both legs. Jean let out a gasp as she saw the impact. She never meant for Davina to get hurt, but she did want her to know the pain she had caused her family.

"God, I pray that you forgive my actions. I know it was wrong, and I repent right here and now. Please let her be okay. This isn't what I want for her. That would be too easy and unfair." Tim held his wife close and refused to let go. He knew this wasn't going to be an easy time for any of them. So many lives had now been turned upside down. How would they come back from this?

Bianca had seen the commotion with Jean and Davina and realized Davina must have done something bad. She also felt like she must have gotten what she deserved. Bianca decided to try to reach out to Robert one more time. She entered the room and found Robert with a small smile on his face. Poor thing, he had no idea about the beatdown his wife just got. Bianca asked Robert if he was okay today, and he said he was. He told her a weight had been lifted from his shoulders. He told her that the hard part was yet to come.

"Did you see my sister out there? Please tell me she didn't find my wife." Bianca only nodded yes that she had indeed found her. "She didn't hurt her, did she?" Bianca only nodded again yes. "Not too bad, she did get a few punches in though."

Just then, Jean walked in. She told Robert that she did hit Davina, and then she told him that she had run out upset. Robert wasn't as upset, as she thought he might have been. "There's more. When she ran out, she was hit by an ambulance. They think her legs are broken but otherwise she should be okay. They took her to do tests." Robert's face turned pale. Even though this woman crushed him, he didn't want any harm to come to her. He knew the punches she took from Jean were more than enough. He had been on the receiving end of those a time or two. Robert grabbed Jean's hand and told her it was going to be okay.

"We will get through this. The only way we know how to, and that is together." Jean squeezed his hand.

"What are we going to tell Mary B? Who's going to tell her about this mess?"

Everyone shook their heads. No one wanted to have that honor. No matter how much they tried to stay on the straight and narrow, the struggle always seemed to find them. Come for them as they may, it only made the family stronger. That strength they would need more than ever to get through this.

Chapter 4

The next few weeks went by in a blur. There was so much pain, so many lies, and a lifetime of hurt to make it through. No one knew just how this would all play out. Neither Robert nor Jean had the guts to speak to Mary B about what had happened. To their knowledge, she still didn't know what dark cloud surrounded the family. Mary B had always been resourceful and anything pertaining to her family, she was always in the know. This current situation was no different. She had always told her children that she had her sources, and she had proven it time and time again.

Mary B chose not to push this situation because there were so many people involved. She wanted her children to come to her when they were ready. It didn't mean that she detested Davina any less or that Tim's father wasn't at fault. There were too many people that could have been blamed, but that wouldn't solve anything. Thinking back, she recalled the beginning of her relationship with William. That story didn't come without its share of secrets in the beginning.

***

Davina's right leg was crushed by the ambulance, and she had undergone several surgeries to repair as much nerve and tendon damage as possible. She had suffered from compartment syndrome which made her feel as if her legs were asleep. The surgeons had to react quickly because if that compartment syndrome lasted, there was the possibility of amputation. Davina had to get several metal screws, pins, and rods added to what was left of her leg.

During all this turmoil, what Davina wanted most was for Robert to be there, but she didn't have the heart to ask for him. She hadn't been able to see her babies, and that too hurt her heart. Davina was more determined to make things right once she healed. She prayed that she would get better. She wasn't a praying woman, but she had her moments. Davina hoped that God would find favor and allow her to at least explain what happened to Robert, so he would understand. She hadn't seen him since he freaked out that awful day their world came crashing down. She knew she couldn't change what had happened in the past, but she knew they could change how they went about the future. She so hoped there would be a future. Davina loved Robert, this she knew without a doubt. She just hated that it took so long to get to this point.

Jean had been keeping her distance from Davina. She hadn't meant for her to get hurt, but she wanted her to understand that she couldn't go around hurting people. Jean's actions led to Davina being seriously hurt and for that she was apologetic. Robert seemed to be handling things okay. He was released from the hospital, and the twins were home with him. So far, Kevin was doing well, and they had high hopes he would be just fine.

Mary B had stepped in as she had so many other times to make sure all the grands were okay. Christian hadn't been heard from since everything had gone down. He had been called away for a conference, and then after that, he had gone away on a mission to Africa. That helped everyone to have some time to adjust to what was to come.

Jean decided it was time to see Davina. She wasn't exactly excited about it but knew it was time. She needed to know why she did it and if she felt bad that she had, or just that she had been caught. When Jean walked into Davina's hospital room, Davina smiled. The reaction shocked them both. Jean just knew that Davina would hate her and hold her responsible for her being hit. Davina knew that Jean would hate her for what she had done to her brother. They were both wrong.

Jean was the first visitor she had, and she had started getting so lonely. Nothing was worse than feeling like you were all alone. The time alone did allow her to think and clear her head. Jean looked at Davina not with hatred but with compassion for the first time since the incident. Looking at Davina as she was at that moment, she saw was a frail, scared young lady. Her life had been disrupted just like everyone else's, even though her actions caused it. Jean wanted to hear her out.

"Davina, listen, I know we haven't spoken since… well, since forever it seems. I'm truly sorry for what happened when you ran out of the hospital. And yeah, I'm sorry for jumping on you. That may not have been the correct way to handle it. But my brother was hurt, and he almost took his life. I had so much hurt and anger built up, and you were the unfortunate target. So, I'm so sorry about that. I pray that you can find it in your heart to forgive me."

"Jean, you got me good, that I won't deny, but I think I had it coming. Although my intentions were not to hurt Robert, I know that I did. For that, I will never forgive myself. I want the chance to explain myself to him and to you, if you would like to listen."

Jean pulled the chair close and sat down. She could see the hurt and sadness in her eyes.

"When Robert and I got together, I was a bit messed up. I was a child without a mother, who had been taken in by one of her men. Joshua tried his best to make sure I was happy, as far as materialistic things. He didn't have kids of his own, so I fit for him. He also had loved my mom, and he thought that was the least he could do. I didn't have anyone to show me what real love was, so I never really connected with anyone like that. When I met Robert, I knew he was different and what I felt was different, but it wasn't until we got married that I truly knew what love was.

"I met Christian before I met Robert actually. We had fun, but it was never meant to be serious. We cared for each other. I never told him about Robert because I didn't see a point at the time, and he never asked. We only saw each other a few times since Robert and I got together. The last time was a day before Robert had come home, upset about you. He wanted me so much. I couldn't deny him, not when I saw the hurt in his eyes. I promise I never thought this would happen. Then out of the blue, a little bit before the twins were born… Matter of fact, it was when you were here and found out you were having twins. Christian saw me. He made contact, and I avoided it as much as I could. I kept putting him off, but he wouldn't stop. All I could do is think about my family and how I didn't want to lose that.

"I will admit to you that I was trying to fake the tests. I didn't want to know the truth. However, truth has a way of coming out whether we want it to or not. So even if I had faked the test and if Kevin had gotten sick, it would have been worse. I know Robert thinks I've betrayed him, and he will probably never forgive me, but as a mother, I did what I thought was right. In hindsight, I couldn't have been more wrong. Lying here day after day, night after night, all I want is my family back."

Jean sat in silence and her heart went out to Davina. She had tried to hate her, but she realized that she wasn't so sure she wouldn't have done the same if she were where Davina was in her life. Jean had been through the fire more than once and she knew all too well what it felt like to have your back against the wall with nowhere to turn. Her heart went out to Davina.

Jean stood up and leaned in to hug Davina, and the tears fell. Jean told her they would get through this, and she would be there to help her. Pulling out her phone, Jean showed Davina pictures she had taken of Kaloni and Kevin. She thought they were getting so big, and it seemed like forever since she had seen them. Davina smiled as she fought back the tears.

"Thank you for that."

"You deserve to see your children. How about later this week, I bring the twins up to see you. They miss you just as much as you do them."

"What about Robert? Won't he have an objection to you bringing them?"

"I know my brother, and he misses you just as much as you do him. He's stubborn, and it will take some time, but he will forgive you. We all make mistakes. It's all in how we pick ourselves up and move on. And it's not too late, we can move on. I'm glad that you trusted me enough to tell me the truth. When you get the chance, tell Robert the truth."

Jean's visit started with a smile, and it ended with one as well. She never thought the truth would feel so good. The burden she had been holding was torture.

Robert had been secretly calling up to the hospital to check on Davina. Even though he was mad at her for her deception, he still loved her with his soul. When they told him she had been hit by the ambulance, his heart skipped a few beats. He would swear to it. It didn't get any better when they said her legs were broken with one being crushed. Then there was the bleeding internally. That wasn't the life he wanted for the mother of his children and the love of his life. Even if she didn't love him back, he loved her with everything in him. He just couldn't believe the whole thing had been a lie. Surely, she had to have felt something for him. Robert thought about the choices he had made, and all of them weren't the best. He had kept a secret from Davina about his drug habit, and he had dragged his sister and Tim into it as well. He had even allowed his children to get out of the house unattended. Thankfully, no harm had come to them. He started second guessing himself. What if he had been honest with her about those things, would she have been honest with him? Would she have felt like he would have had her back? These questions he didn't have the answer to, but he felt confident that one day he would.

Jean held true to her promise to bring the babies to see Davina. Jean understood why she felt the need to protect her family. She just wished it hadn't come at such a price. Robert was being super stubborn; he said he wasn't ready to see Davina just yet. He did tell Jean he had been calling to check on her though.

"I knew you couldn't resist. You're trying to be stubborn, but you can't deny you love and still care."

"Of course I care; she's the mother of my children. She will forever be my rib." Jean smiled to herself. She knew that she just had to give him time, and he would come around.

***

Tim had been upset by this whole ordeal. He was just thinking he was ready to get to know his father. Although all of this wasn't Christian's fault, and he knew that, it didn't make it any easier. What would Jean think of his father, of him? What if she thought he would do the same as his father and be careless. Tim wondered if he was destined to follow in his footsteps also. He was trying to be true to Jean. They had been through so much, but what if it got to be too much and he decided to bail on her? He hated his dad for making him feel this way. To make things worse, his dad was gone. Everything blew up and he was gone. He didn't have to face the questions or the wrath of Mary B. Tim thought his dad was lucky to avoid that. Hopefully, by the time he returned, things would be on their way back to normal.

***

After seeing the children, Davina felt she needed to get better, so she could go home. She had been depressed and didn't realize just how much until she saw the children. Davina knew that she missed them, but her eyes watered at the sight of them. Although Robert wasn't ready to forgive her, he had sent them with a few cards, a stuffed teddy bear, and some balloons. Her heart melted when she saw them. Kevin walked over to her bed with one single rose behind his back. He told her that it was from daddy. She knew all hope wasn't lost. He had always given her a single rose whenever they argued. That was his own way of saying he apologized. She just had to wait it out, and she was up to the challenge.

Davina had a struggle ahead of her. She had been scheduled to do therapy, but she was having a hard time. The therapist didn't want to rush her because she had suffered a great deal with her injuries. The feeling in her right leg was coming and going, mostly going. She would get frustrated and upset and refuse to continue therapy. This whole learning to walk again was for the birds.

"How can I walk if I can't even feel my leg?" She became a little depressed and agitated. When Jean would come by, she could tell Davina didn't want to be bothered.

Robert had continued his secretive calling up to the hospital, and he grew concerned when they told him she wasn't able to put pressure on her right leg. He decided it was time to pay her a visit. He realized it wasn't about him, but about her getting better. Robert knew she had no one and had been at the hospital for weeks without anyone there to support her. Although he wasn't quite ready to act as if nothing had happened, he knew it was time to talk to her. He thought deep down, once they had a conversation, she could focus on recovering. Robert had to admit the children were wearing him out. He never imagined raising the children on his own.

Robert stopped by the gift shop when he arrived at the hospital to get a single rose for Vina. As he stepped onto the elevator, he bumped into Bianca. They smiled and spoke to each other. Robert was glad he had opted to dress nicely and add a dash of cologne for this trip. He just wanted Bianca to know he wasn't some druggy who didn't want to live.

"How have you been, Robert? You're looking good… well, I mean much better than the last time I saw you."

"I'm doing much better than I was at the time. I'm still just getting adjusted. A lot of things changed in my world. How about you? How is Lucas? I got his name right, didn't I?"

Bianca smiled. "Yeah, you got it right. Lucas is doing well. He proposed last week. We're thinking about dates."

Just then, the elevator stopped, and Robert moved to get off. He looked back at her and told her, "You know, I appreciate everything you did for me when I was here. I know you were only trying to help, and you did. I'm happy that Lucas realized what type of young lady you are and decided to put a ring on it." They both smiled and said their goodbyes. Bianca liked the way this family stuck together.

Standing in Davina's doorway, he looked in through the closed door. She looked so frail and broken, unlike his little fireball he had grown to love. He knocked on the door, and Davina looked over and saw him. She immediately tried to fix her hair and wipe her eyes. She didn't want him to see her crying.

"What's wrong, Vina Bina?" Robert asked as he walked over to her bed.

He instinctively bent down and placed a kiss on her chapped lips. Davina wasn't expecting that and immediately put her hand to her lips and said, "Sorry, didn't mean to cut you up." Robert smiled. Normally, he would have clowned around with her, but he just smiled. He wanted to do nothing more than grab her up and hold her close and tell her it would be okay. He almost forgot the rose he had in his hand, but he gave it to her, and she broke down in tears. "I thought it was a mistake when Kevin gave the other one to me. I thought maybe you did it just to be kind. But I did start to hope that it was real. I've been lying here trying to think about what I've done and what I could have done. All my answers come back to you. I should have been honest and trusted you. For that, I have no excuse. I just went into defense mode. I didn't give you the option to love me or be there for me. That's something I will always have to live with."

"Davina, you were my world. I've made my own share of mistakes, and I didn't give you a choice either. I've got so much to tell you, but I don't want to stress you." Davina was just happy that Robert had come to see her. That meant he was willing to try to get past all that had happened.

"Robert, I'm glad that you're here, no matter the capacity. We were friends before anything else, and I value that more than life itself now." Robert pulled the chair closer to the bed and grabbed her hand. He brought it to his mouth and kissed it, winking at her. In that moment, all was right with the world.

Chapter 5

Robert stayed with her for hours and to him, it only felt like moments. He hadn't realized just how much he missed her. They talked about her legs and what was going on with them. Davina told him the right one was being stubborn and causing her problems. She told him that another surgery was probably in her future. They needed to try to repair the nerves and tendons. The first surgery didn't do what they expected. The surgery alone was a big risk; she could inadvertently become paralyzed. Robert's face showed his concern. When she looked at him, he tried to change it, but she had already seen the worry.

"It's okay, Robert. I have to try it. I have to try to get myself better."

"I'm sorry this happened to you, my sweet Vina Bina. I never wanted you to be hurt."

"I know. I don't blame anyone for this. It's called karma, and it has its own way of making things right. Jean and I have talked, and I had to tell her that this wasn't on her either. Sometimes we go through things to appreciate what we have. I took you for granted. I knew you loved me, and I just took it for granted and didn't treasure it like I should have. The Bible says the husband is supposed to provide, right?" She smiled at him then.

"Yeah, to a degree, and I tried my best to give you everything you wanted and to provide for the children. I started doing the overtime, and then it wasn't good because I started being away from home too much. I turned to drugs to help me get through the days. I felt like there was something wrong with us, but I thought I was over thinking stuff."

"Wait, wait a minute, you were doing drugs? How did I not see that? I was caught up in my own crap, I was too blind to see." "Not totally your fault. I did a pretty good job of covering it up. Then when that stuff came to a head, I couldn't deal. I went to my spot, and I just wanted what I normally got. It was nothing major, just some uppers, to stimulate me a little. To just to get my mind off the craziness. My guy was out, and he gave me some heroin instead. That was the worst mistake of my life. I had no idea what I was doing. I just wanted to not feel the pain. I wasn't trying to kill myself, although it didn't seem like that. I know you were only trying to be there for me when I was hospitalized, and I was wrong for turning you away and treating you that way. I just wasn't ready to see you and admit that I had failed you."

Davina knew this was only the beginning of a long road ahead. She was optimistic they would find their way back to each other sooner than later. As luck would have it, she couldn't have been more right.

At that moment, Robert smiled at her and looked at his watch. He had been there with her for most of the day. He thought back to when they met. They would talk for hours and hours. He couldn't get enough of her then and the same remained true. She was his rib after all. The one made just for him. Sometimes it just took going the long way around to realize what was right in front of you.

Robert smiled to himself at the thought of Mary B's famous words. She had used them so many times as they were growing up.

***

Bianca and Lucas had started planning their wedding. The one thing she hadn't planned on was getting pregnant. She was almost nine months and wasn't showing but a little. Bianca had found out that it was a little girl.

During their many talks, Lucas had made it clear that he didn't want any children now or in the future. That was one of the many things they had agreed on. They both knew they wanted to get up and go anytime they wanted, without worrying about children. Bianca was spoiled, and she didn't think she wanted to share that with anyone. She wasn't trying to be selfish, but she knew her limits. She didn't want to be responsible for mistreating another life. Bianca knew she couldn't abort the baby, so she had decided it would be best to give the baby up. She had become a nurse to save others. The reality was that she had to find a safe home for her unborn daughter. The more she thought about it the more she felt like she had found the right one. She just needed to make sure.

Lucas didn't know that Bianca was pregnant. It had been about six months since he had seen her; he was stationed overseas at the time. He wouldn't be back for another four months by the time all the paperwork was finalized. She hated deceiving him, but he was very clear on what he wanted. Bianca was careful when they skyped not to let him see too much of her. She feared he would see the changes her body had gone through.

Through her talks with Robert, she had learned so much about his family, especially when he was trying hard to avoid telling her about himself. She had learned all about the God-fearing Mary B, there wasn't anything she wouldn't do for her family. Bianca learned that Jean had overcome so many obstacles and had been doing well. She was possibly the strongest woman Bianca knew of. Here she was feeling selfish, not wanting to have any children, while this woman fought so hard to be there for hers. Bianca admired Jean from a distance. She saw how much she loved her brother and was determined to help him and his wife work things out. She seemed to have been doing a good job at it.

Bianca had been checking in on Davina, just to make sure she was okay. They had become pretty good friends. She had sensed Davina was a little hesitant to open up at first, but she finally did. Bianca needed a friend more than even she knew. During her talks with Davina, she noticed that she too talked about her sister-in-law with such admiration. That secured her thoughts that she would approach Jean about taking her baby.

"Hey, Jean. I'm Bianca. I was your brother's nurse for a few days while he was here before. I was wondering if you would be interested in taking my baby." She knew this sounded crazy, but she worked her nerves up and rehearsed what to say. She had to decide soon, she had only a month to go before the baby was due.

One day while Jean was visiting Davina, Bianca decided it was time to ask her. She saw Jean walking out of Davina's room, and she quickly approached her.

"Hey, excuse me. You're Jean, right? Robert's sister?" Jean nodded but her face turned pale.

Her thoughts went to Robert. "Did something happen to my brother?"

"Oh no, ma'am. I'm sorry for asking in that way. I just need to talk to you about something. It has nothing to do with your brother. I know this is going to sound crazy, but I've been watching you for some time now. Well, since your brother was brought in. I promise not in a creepy way." She saw the look of puzzlement on Jean's face. "Maybe I should start from the beginning. Do you have a moment to talk? I promise not to keep you too long." Jean nodded that she had time to chat. Bianca's hand went to her belly without her noticing it, but Jean did.

"Again, I'm sorry to bother you and I appreciate your time. My name is Bianca, and I was one of the nurses that tended to your brother during his stay here. I've become pretty good friends with Davina. As I've listened to them both talk about you, I feel like you're an angel here on earth. I hope you don't mind but your brother told me some of the things you've endured. Mind you, he only told me about you, so he wouldn't have to talk about himself. He simply deflected. Then Davina shared how out of everyone, you were the one pulling for her to get better, although she has a way to go. You came to see her, and you actually listened without judging her." Bianca laughed aloud. "I also saw when you went to her tail, the same day she ended up here. She and I both know it was out of love for your brother. Anyway, to make a long story short, I have something to ask you and you'll probably think me crazy. I pray you don't think me a horrible person, but I would like to know if you would be willing to take my baby." Jean's eyes dropped to her tummy. She saw a small bulge, but of course, she didn't have much to go from.

"How far along would you be, Bianca?"

"I'm almost nine months ma'am." Jean was in disbelief but then, she recalled her own pregnancy with Miles.

"Why are you trying to give up your child, my dear?"

"How much time do you have? My fiancé is overseas currently. We're planning to get married shortly after he returns, which should be in about four months give or take. He and I had agreed that we didn't want any children, and I honestly don't. Before he left, we slipped up and now here I am pregnant, eight months to be exact. Lucas doesn't know about the baby. I think he would be furious. If you take the baby, when he comes back, he wouldn't have to know."

Jean looked baffled. "You mean you're not going to tell him he has a child?"

"No, Miss Jean. You don't understand. He was very adamant about not having any children. We were just going to spend the rest of our lives loving each other."

This will be a marriage based on lies. It won't work. "How about you tell him, and then we talk about what I can do to help you move on. I hadn't thought about any more children. My husband keeps us supplied in that department. I will help you though. Not sure how just yet."

Bianca told her she would think about telling him but didn't want to mess up what they had. Jean told her, "Honesty is the best policy. You may think it's easier to deceive him or to just get rid of the child, but there are more people to consider. Do you really think he will be all right with knowing he has a child out there in the world that he doesn't know?" Bianca honestly couldn't answer that, but she knew she couldn't take care of a child. She assured Jean she would try her best to find out.

The next morning, she thought she would test the waters with Lucas when they skyped. "Lucas, would it be so bad if we did start a family?" she asked halfway into the conversation. You would have thought that she had asked him to kill someone.

"B, we've talked about that before, on several occasions. You know I lost my parents when I was young, and I don't want a child to have to deal with that. It's a lonely and horrible existence. That was until we found each other. I was grateful we shared the same dreams and had so much in common. You were a godsend. I've been on my own since I was seventeen, and I love it. There isn't anything to tie me down to any one place. When the military says I need to go wherever, I'm free to go without feeling regrets of leaving some children behind and being away from them. Why are we talking about this again? Is something going on? Did you change your mind? I know I've been gone for six months. That did give you time to think."

"No, baby. I just wanted to make sure you hadn't changed your mind. So, what would happen if we slipped up and got pregnant? You know I can't abort a child."

"B, we aren't going to get to that point. If you take your pills, we have no worries. You have been taking them, right?"

"Of course, Lucas." That's the crazy part; she had been careful and made sure she took her pill everyday religiously. That didn't help, she still got pregnant. His reaction was just as she thought it would be. She was sure she was making the right choice by not telling him and finding a home for their unborn child. That home she was sure would be with Jean. She just had to convince Jean of this.

She figured she would give Jean a little time to let what she had asked of her to sink in. Bianca knew they didn't have a lot of time. If the baby came on time, she had approximately three weeks. Three short weeks to ensure her child had a home and would be cared for. She hadn't told Jean that she would set up an account to provide for the child. She felt like that wouldn't really make a difference.

Bianca ran into Jean a few days later at the hospital, and she asked her again to please take and care for her child. "Did you talk to your fiancé about the baby?"

"I did in a roundabout way. I asked him what would happen if we were to accidentally get pregnant, and he kindly reminded me of his world when he lost both parents at the age of seventeen. That was a life he just couldn't, well, wouldn't hand down to his child."

"You do know for adoption you have to have the daddy's signature as well."

"I thought I would just kind of hand her over to you, and I will sign whatever you want me to, to say that you are her guardian. I would give up any parental rights. You just say the word and it is done. I will say I don't know who the father is."

"You know that I will have to talk to my husband about all of this. I hadn't mentioned it because I thought you would snap to your senses. I wasn't expecting you to really go through with this."

"I am thinking with a clear head. I promise you that. I may not want her, but I want to make sure she will be cared for and loved. For some reason, I feel like you can give her that. The one thing I can't, unconditional love. Please talk to Tim. If I need to plead my case to him as well, I will. I'm begging you at this point."

With everything that Jean had been through, she knew she couldn't just let the baby go to anyone. She didn't know why but she felt compelled to help this young lady, the way others had always been there to help her. What would Mary B do in this situation? She smiled to herself. Mary B would be like 'I didn't make that baby, but go on, give her here. I'll do the best I can.' So now came the true test and that was talking to Tim about it. It would be an adjustment for everyone, including the babies she had already.

It was still a shock to Jean to believe that someone wanted her to take their child and that they believed she would be a good mother. Now to her four, she was a pretty good mom, but it wasn't always that way. Miles knew all too well how bad of a parent she could be, but even he had forgiven her for her lack of parenting skills in her early years. She had been trying her best to make up for it. She didn't take lightly the demons she had to fight almost daily. There were so many questions: what if Bianca wasn't being truthful to her or with Lucas? What would happen if they wanted the baby girl back? Those were questions Jean didn't have the answers to. If she followed her heart, it told her to take the baby from Bianca and raise her as her own. If the time came when they wanted her back, they would cross that bridge, then.

Jean knew that like every decision she would make, there were always a few people to consult. She knew Mia wouldn't mind; she would have a girl to play with. The boys might be a little harder to convince. Tim would probably ask her if she were crazy.

"Don't you think we have enough?" she could almost hear him say. She thought it best to talk to Mary B and William. They would give her their most honest opinion. Even when Jean didn't ask for it, they were always in full supply of advice.

Chapter 6

Tim had been preoccupied trying to reach his dad, to no avail. Whether he wanted to admit it or not, he was beginning to worry about him. He tried calling Jeff to see if he had heard from him. No such luck there. Tim decided he would try to call him again tomorrow. He hadn't shared with Jean that he had been trying to contact him. With all that had happened, he just felt like his dad could probably use a friend. When Jean told Tim she needed to talk to him, he didn't really understand the importance of the conversation. That was until it began.

Jean asked Tim to meet her at their favorite restaurant Dot's Place on his way home that night. Tim agreed, and he was there waiting for Jean when she arrived. After being seated, Jean wasted no time. As she reached for Tim's hand, he smiled and asked, "What is it, baby? Are we expecting again?"

Jean's expression changed to one of amusement, how could he know that and why would he assume that of all things? "Not exactly. Why did you think that was what this conversation is about?"

"I just assumed. You know, we've been popping them out every few years or so." Tim smiled as he said that. Jean couldn't do anything but agree. She thought how much she loved his smile. Shaking her head, she snapped herself back to the real reason for this dinner.

"Would you be okay if we did have another baby?"

"Are we? Are we having another baby?"

"Well, that's what I wanted to talk to you about." Jean began telling Tim about Bianca and the conversations they had been having.

Tim asked her, "Why did she pick us of all the people in this town?" Jean told him she thought we would take care of her and love her as we would our very own.

"The thing is though, she's going to be giving birth any day now. She was already at the eight-month mark a few weeks ago. I don't owe her anything, but I remember how people, including you, were there for me when I was lost. It may or may not be permanent, but we know that going in. That won't stop me from providing and nurturing her as best I can. Financially, I think we'll be okay. It would be an adjustment for the children as well. We can talk to them tonight and make sure they don't have any issues. We'll be honest with them and tell them we're considering taking a child in to give her a good, loving home. She'll be treated just as if she was our own."

"Jeannie, it seems you've already made the decision. Are you sure about all of this? Are you healthy enough?" He wanted to make sure she wasn't going through the depression episodes again. He tried not to ask her about the medication as much anymore; he didn't want her to think that he felt her less of a mom or a woman.

"Tim, I'm fine. I've been taking the medication as directed. I'd rather take the little girl instead of her being taken in by someone who would neglect or abuse her. I'm not saying I'm the best mom, but you're the best dad." She thought that would surely get him to see reason. And she was right. He smiled and squeezed her hand. She knew the answer was indeed yes. She felt a flutter in her tummy. She passed it off as it was her nerves. Jean pulled out her phone to call Bianca to arrange a meeting to discuss the details.

Jean called Mary B later that night after they had spoken with the children. Mary B, without hesitation, said it's about time. I've been dreaming of fish for two days now. Jean corrected Mary B and told her the child was going to be adopted. Mary B said you might want to check it out. She told Jean she had never been wrong. Jean had to agree. All night, Jean tossed and turned, unable to shake what Mary B had said. Finally, sleep came searching for her.

The next morning, Jean found a pregnancy test kit she had for a while and decided it wouldn't hurt to verify what Mary B had said. Besides, she would have loved nothing better than to tell Mary B she was finally wrong about something. Jean didn't get that chance. It seemed as if hours passed by as she watched that stick and then, she finally saw the plus sign. Tears fell from her eyes, as she wondered what she had done. Her raced and without warning, she hit the floor. "Thump!" Tim ran into the bathroom and saw her lying on the floor.

"Jeannie, Jeannie, are you okay?" Jean slowly nodded yes. "Do you need to go to the doctor? What's going on? What's wrong, baby?" He was asking her so many questions at once. Jean's mind couldn't process them as quickly. Tim's eyes found her hand, and more importantly, what was in it.

Tears rolled down Jean's eyes as Tim reached and took the test from her hand. "Is this real? Is this happening right now?"

"Tim, I just found out. I didn't suspect until last night after talking to Momma. She told me to check and so, this morning I did. I know this makes it harder to accept another woman's child if we're bringing one of our own into the world. I totally understand if you think it's too much."

Tim, who had been silent for a moment, softened his face. "We can do whatever you want, baby. If you feel like it's the right thing to do, then we will. We will manage, we always do."

Jean hugged Tim and knew this man loved her more than life itself. She was thankful for him and his love. It had saved her many times in the last few years. Jean smiled and giggled a little.

Tim looked at her. "What's that for?"

"I've got to call Momma and tell her she was right again." They both laughed. Helping his wife up off the floor, Tim asked her again if she was okay. Jean assured him she was. At that moment, Jean heard her phone ringing but couldn't get to it in time. Jean figured she would check her phone once she finished getting ready for her day.

***

Bianca had awakened in the middle of the night with some bad cramps. She had tried calling Jean, but she didn't answer so after a few hours of pain, she drove herself to the hospital in the next town. As she was getting out of her car, she felt something running down her leg. Looking down, she realized her water had broken. A nurse helped her get inside and into a wheelchair.

"Are you pregnant?" Looking down, she saw Bianca's clothes were soaked. They rushed her back to check her and the baby's vitals. Once they were stable, Bianca tried calling Jean again. Still no answer so she left her a message. She only hoped she would get it before the baby came. Bianca didn't want to admit it, but she was scared and wanted to have someone there with her.

Reaching for her phone, Bianca called Jean again. This time, she answered.

"Hello Jean, this is Bianca. I'm sorry to keep calling but, the baby is coming." Bianca yelled out in pain, a contraction came without any warning.

"Where are you?"

"St Joseph's in Marshdale."

"I know the one. I will be there as soon as I can. Hold on, I'm coming." After calling Mary B to stay with the children, Jean and Tim were on their way to Marshdale. Jean called Bianca back "How are you holding up?"

"I don't know how women do this. I've never felt this pain before, and I don't want to go through it again." Bianca's breathing became labored.

"Come on, Bianca. Take slow breaths. Keep it together. I'm almost there." Bianca was grateful for a familiar voice and did as she was told. Jean stayed on the phone with her the whole way to the hospital. Lying in the bed, Bianca looked like a helpless little girl herself. Jean understood at that moment, Bianca was doing the best thing she could for her child.

The contractions kept coming and soon the nurse came and said it was time. The little unborn child's heartbeat was starting to spike. They didn't want to waste any time and she becomes stressed. Bianca asked Jean if she would stay with her during delivery, and of course, she couldn't deny her that. Jean held her hand during every push, and Jean felt like she had given birth herself when she heard Kim's cries for the first time. She knew that was her baby girl. Jean looked down at the beautiful baby girl and smiled and cried.

"Do you want to see her?" she asked Bianca. She shook her head no.

"Is she beautiful?"

"You should look at her and see for yourself, and to make sure this is what you want to do."

"I'm afraid if I look, her face will haunt me, or I will change my mind."

"You can always visit her, or if you change your mind and want to keep her, you can do so now."

"That's not going to happen. I'm not equipped to be a mother, and I'm okay with that."

"Bianca, I almost told you today that I couldn't do it. I just found out that I'm pregnant, and I didn't know how it would work out. Tim has been amazing through everything. He said we will be just fine. I won't lie to this little girl. I just don't want to confuse her, so when the time comes, she will know that you loved her but wanted her to be with someone who would love her just as much."

"I'm so thankful for you and Tim both. Without you, I would have been lost. Congratulations on the other addition that you're going to have. Are you sure you'll be able to handle Kim along with the new baby also?"

"God will provide a way, he always does." Although Jean seemed confident on the outside, on the inside, she was all nerves.

Bianca kept to her word and didn't see her baby girl the whole time she was in the hospital with her. She was determined to move on now that she had found a good home for her. Bianca knew she could trust Jean and Tim to take care of her daughter as if she were their very own. After her release from the hospital, Bianca planned to head out of town. She had already told Lucas that she was going to visit her mom and dad. So that would keep him from suspecting anything. She intended to stay with her mom and dad until Lucas returned.

***

Jean hadn't talked to Mary B since the night before Bianca gave birth to Kim. She had so much to talk to her about.

"Momma, guess what?"

"You actually found out you were pregnant, child? I haven't seen you or talked to you since I told you to get that checked. Now what is this about taking on a baby that doesn't belong to you or your husband?"

"Well, Momma, we are indeed pregnant. I don't know how you always seem to know, but you do. We have a brand-new baby girl that will be introduced to the family tomorrow when she is released from the hospital. Stop looking at me like that. Long story short, do you remember Robert's nurse when he overdosed? She just gave birth a few days ago. She's supposed to be getting married to her fiancé and neither of them wants children. And yes, she was taking birth control pills, but something happened. Apparently, God had other plans. We'll be taking the baby in as our own, but with no lies, and in nine months or so, we will welcome yet another baby into the house. Momma, if we, Tim and I, didn't think it was for the best, we wouldn't have taken on the responsibility."

Mary B just shook her head. "I pray you are right, child. You know I often worry about you and if you are okay. I know you still have your demons and all."

"Momma, I'm okay. I wouldn't do it if I wasn't sure." Jean hated that everyone seemed to still treat her with kid gloves as if she was fragile. She would just have to prove to them she wasn't.

Chapter 7

As the weeks passed, Tim was getting more and more concerned about Christian. All his calls were still going unanswered, and his phone was going straight to voicemail. No one had heard from him, including Davina. He decided it was time to voice his concern to Jean.

Over dinner, the last night before they brought their baby girl home, they enjoyed a nice family dinner. Tim asked Miles, Dayshaun, Joseph, and Mia if they were all okay one final time about them bringing another little girl home. Miles and Dayshaun understood, but Mia and Joseph were a little too young. They just smiled because everyone else was.

After dinner, Tim asked if Jean would go for a walk with him. "Our last night of freedom," he joked. They had been down this road before but never with it being someone else's child. Tim admitted he was a little worried but not enough not to try it. He also told Jean that he was getting worried about his dad. He couldn't believe it… he used the word dad. Tim told Jean that he had reached out to Davina to see if she had heard from him.

Davina told him her last contact was via text. Christian was in Mexico doing some mission work. That had been some time ago though, so she was starting to get a little concerned for him also. Although, she didn't want to voice it because she didn't want Robert to think she felt anything other than friendship for him. They had made some progress and she was happy about that.

Tim had tried calling Christian's boss but even he hadn't heard from him. He too thought it strange but said that sometimes that was just how Christian was. Jean suggested that maybe Tim should go to Mexico if he felt that strongly about it.

"I'm not going to leave you with the children and with a new baby too. I will give it some time to see if he responds. I just wanted you to know that I was finally willing to forgive him and move on, and now he is gone. It just makes me think back to when I was younger, and he abandoned us then. Now he has a mess here and he's gone, as if it doesn't matter."

"Tim, be patient. He didn't seem to me like he wasn't affected by all of this. He was trying to resolve it before things got bad. Davina told me he had in fact made several attempts to get it handled. If he didn't plan on being around, I'm sure he wouldn't have gotten tested."

"Yeah ,Jeannie, I know, I know… But it still just makes me sick on my stomach. I actually thought he was changing."

"Tim, you can't fault him for being human. He and Davina both did that. I know you're feeling bad for Robert, but he's coping with it all. He knows his wife was a part of that choice. And things will be different for us all. Our family dynamics is not like your average family. Please, for us all, baby, take it easy on him, and remember it wasn't all on him."

Tim pulled Jean close. He loved her always but there were times that he just loved her more than life itself. This was one of those times. Through all she had been through, she still managed to find the bright spot. It was easy for her to forgive, and he loved that about her. He also felt like sometimes she shouldn't have been so forgiving, especially when it came to Fred.

Tim's phone rang, snapping him out of his thoughts.

"Tim, son, it's me Christian. I'm just now seeing that you were calling me. There was an accident, and I was out of it for several weeks."

"What! What happened!"

"The transport van I was on, turned over and for days, no one found me and two other passengers. The van flipped, and we ended up in a ravine. I'm okay, just a broken collarbone. I will live. As soon as I can fly, I will be coming back. I know there is something's that must be worked out with Kevin. I promise you that I will do right by him. If that means hanging back, so they can do what needs to be done, I will do it. I don't want to jeopardize the relationship I was trying to build back with you and Jeff and destroy another life in the process."

Tim was relieved that he had heard from his dad, but he told him to get his rest. They would talk about it when he got back, and he told him to keep in touch. Christian agreed that he would and thanked him for being concerned.

Christian hadn't told him the whole story. He had been driving and started having a seizure. He lost control of the vehicle. The doctors said he was lucky that he and the others were still alive. The doctor said it was a mild seizure, but if it had been a full-blown one, he and the others wouldn't have survived.

Christian had never had seizures before. So, as a doctor, this didn't go over well with him. It didn't help when he was told he had meningitis. He had it for some time, since he had come back from one of his trips. Christian didn't even remember being bitten by a mosquito, but there were so many other things he had been frightened of being bitten by. The hours he had been working, he hadn't even noticed that he had been having bad headaches.

After the doctors did the lumbar puncture, they confirmed their suspicion of it being meningitis. They did a CT scan and some blood cultures. The doctors didn't like the swelling they saw in his brain. They were positive they could treat it, and he was hopeful that by the time his collarbone had healed, this nightmare would also be over.

Christian hated not telling Tim the truth. He had hoped that they could resolve their differences. He wanted a relationship with his sons more than anything, including Kevin but not at the risk of causing issues for Davina. He had no doubt that Davina and Robert would take care of his youngest son. He just didn't want Kevin to grow up hating him like Jeff and Tim. One thing at a time, Chris, one thing at a time. You will have your chance to make everything right. Just make the most of it, when you get it.

Tim was happy to have finally spoken with Christian, and he was glad to hear he was all right. He was glad he took his wife's advice to try to forgive him and move forward. Jean had seen the relief in Tim's face as he spoke with Christian, and she knew they would be okay. Tim was like a kid who hadn't spoken with his dad in months, and he was happy. That was all Jean had ever wanted for Tim. This was a new beginning

***

Davina had the surgery to repair her nerve damage, but it wasn't as successful as she or the doctors had hoped. Robert seemed just as frustrated. Davina had been in the hospital for a while now. During surgery, one of her nerves was damaged further. They tried to repair it while they were already in her leg, but it didn't work. She came out of the surgery with her right leg paralyzed. The doctors couldn't tell her how long she would be in this condition. Robert told Davina he would always be there, and they would figure it all out.

"Robert, I appreciate you trying to stick by me, but you don't have to. You don't owe me anything. How am I supposed to come home and take care of my family? I feel helpless, even though this was my idea to go ahead with the surgery. I guess I just thought it would go correctly."

"We both did. But it will get better and even if for some reason it doesn't, we'll be fine. We've been through worse. Besides, I think the kids are missing you, I'm no you, that's for sure."

"I'm certain you're being an amazing dad to the twins. The thoughts of them and you keep me going. The doctor said in a few weeks I can go home. If the paralysis doesn't go away, I can still do rehab as outpatient. They said that could possibly strengthen the nerves and the tendons. They did also say I can't overdo it."

Robert knew his wife wouldn't follow those orders. He had to admit he was ready for her to come home. He made a mental note to speak to the doctors tomorrow to see if there was any way possible she could be released earlier.

"I love you so much, Robert, and I'm truly sorry for everything."

"I know, Vina. That's why I'm here. We'll get through this, I promise you that. If I've learned anything during the last few months is that prayer changes things. My mom tried to instill that in us as children, and we often retaliated against it, but the words still rang true. I've prayed so much in these last few weeks that I know God is tired of hearing my voice."

Robert believed his words to be true. There was nothing any one could have told him to make him believe otherwise. He wouldn't rest until she was home and in better spirits.

The last few days seemed to have gone by in a blur. Tim and Jean were getting used to having a baby at home. This was a change for the other children as well. Bianca had stayed true to her word. There was an account set up for the baby, to help provide for her. She still hadn't seen the baby, but she called Jean to tell her she was leaving town within a few weeks, and she wanted to sign any documents they needed so there wouldn't be any issues as far as insurance or their parental rights. Tim had been preoccupied with making sure Christian was okay, that he left that part to Jean. He told her to just let him know where he needed to be and when.

Jean knew Tim wasn't taking the news from Christian too well. She decided she would dip into their savings and send him to Mexico, so he could be with him. It seemed like what he needed, even though he tried not to admit it. She didn't think he needed to continue sacrificing his peace of mind to make sure he was there for her and the kids. Jean knew she couldn't just say, "Hey baby, why don't you go visit your dad." She knew she had to go ahead and purchase the ticket first herself and just present it to him.

Tim reluctantly agreed, however he was thankful to have Jean as his wife.

***

Christian had been required to stay at the hospital, so he could receive the antibiotics intravenously. He was also placed on a heart monitor, and because of his collarbone, he had his arm in a sling. He was at the mercy of the hospital and was shocked when Tim walked through the door. That wasn't something he was prepared for, but he couldn't contain his smile. He had to admit he was glad to see him. This let him know he was making strides with their relationship, and for that he was grateful.

"What are you doing here, Tim?"

"I was concerned and wanted to make sure you were really okay. You know, sometimes people say they good and really they're not."

"Tim, listen, I appreciate it, but you really didn't have to fly all the way down here."

"It's okay. We have a lot going on at home. I could use a little break. Besides, Jean kind of forced me, and you know what she says goes."

Trying to keep things light, Christian kept the conversation focused on Tim. "What's going on at home? Is everything okay?"

"Everything is good; we are having another baby in about eight months. We just added another a little addition, a little girl." Tim noticed that Christian had a look of confusion on his face. "It's a long story. We took in a newborn baby girl. Her mom didn't want her, and her dad doesn't even know. Yeah, I know her life is already starting off crazy, but that's where we come in. We can give her the best life for as long as we can."

Christian looked at his son, not as a son, but as a man for one of the first times since they had been in contact. He thought to himself, this man sitting here with him had grown and advanced far beyond his belief. His heart wasn't bitter, and he gave so much of himself to and for others.

"How did you and Jean meet, if I may ask?"

"You do know I realize you're just trying to keep the subject off you, right?" Christian just laughed and shook his head no. "My wife has been through some rough stuff in her life. I met her just when I needed her most, although she often says it was the other way around.

She had been through a horrible experience, and she was at the hospital I was working at. At the time, I just tried to be a good friend. That turned into admiration and then I fell in love with her and her son. But I remained professional until she left the hospital, and it just went from there. I met her not long after we lost Mom. You know she never said a bad word about you. You were the love of mom's life."

"Son, she was my greatest love too, even though you may not believe it. I promise you that it's true. I was at her funeral, and it hurt my heart that you and your brother had to deal with all that stuff alone. There were many days I wanted to tell you all what really happened, but I realized the damage was already done. You know I messed up and made some bad choices in my life. It warms my heart to see that you didn't take on my bad habits. Jean is lucky to have you in her life."

"No, Dad, that's where you are wrong. I'm lucky to have her. Her strength gives me strength, and there's no place I'd rather be. There's no other woman who can do for me what she does. I'm thankful every day that she chose me."

Christian smiled. He was proud of this man standing before him. "Tim, I wasn't completely honest with you when I called you. Yes, my collarbone is broken, but I caused the accident. I had a seizure and lost control of the vehicle and nearly killed two others. Thank God they lived. That would have been something I would have had to live with for the rest of my days. It's bad enough that they were hurt due to me."

"Seizures? Has this happened before?"

"No, I have also been diagnosed with meningitis. It's not looking too good. The doctors believe they can get it under control. There's some swelling in my brain, that's what this IV is for."

"So, why didn't you just tell me this over the phone? You don't have to go through things by yourself, not any more at least. How long before you can go home?"

"They want me to stay a few weeks just to make sure the antibiotics are doing their job and to monitor my heart as well as this swelling in my head. Once they give me the all clear, I will be on the next flight out. I do appreciate you coming down here, but I will be fine."

"Yeah, I know you will. I've practiced killing you a thousand times in my dreams and they never worked." Christian looked amused. "Yeah, I was an angry kid. I had to step up and be the man before my time and for that, I hated you. To be honest, it wasn't until I met Jean and saw you again that I could let that part go. That's what she does for me. She literally makes me a better man. I see our family and I know I have to be better for those boys of ours, and for the little girls. I need to be an example of the type of man they should be looking for later in life."

Christian could only smile. His absence didn't hurt him, but it made him stronger. He was truly proud of him. "Well, I must say I'm glad that killing me in your dreams didn't work, although I know in your mind, I deserved it. Again, thank you for the concern, but I'm going to be all right. You can go home and be with Jean and the babies. I know you have pictures, may I see? Is Jean okay with you being here?"

"My wife is super woman in disguise. She's the reason I'm here. She knew I was feeling a bit uneasy, and she handled it all. I woke up and my clothes were packed. She was like, 'Shower and get dressed. We have to go.' We arrived at the airport, she kissed me, said see you later, and here I am."

"She sounds a lot like your mom. She took care of me like that too. A woman like that is hard to come by. I see why you cherish her."

"Well, Dad, I'm going to get a room and get situated. I need to call my wife and check on the children. You know, to make sure she's still breathing. When I come back, maybe we can talk about all this mess with Davina and how we will handle it going forward. She and Robert are working things out, so we don't want to disrupt that. I guess you'll have to finally meet Mary B and William, Jean's parents. I've not talked about you a lot because I was still unsure about everything, and then when all that stuff with Davina took place, it wasn't the time to make introductions."

"Yeah, I don't think that would have been the appropriate time to say, 'Hello, I'm his dad, and the father of your son's wife's baby.'"

"Yeah, William might have tried to hurt you, but Mary B is the one to watch out for."

"So… you're still determined to stick around, huh? I'm really okay."

"I will see you later, sir. Do you need anything? Oh, and I will show you pictures of the kids when I get back." Just like that, Christian's life has taken a turn in the right direction. It's crazy how a tragedy could bring people closer together.

Chapter 8

"Jean, I'm sorry, babe, that I didn't call when I landed. Yes, I'm safe. I just checked into the hotel room. Yes, he's fine. He sends his love to you. I told him I would be introducing him to Mary B and William soon." Tim couldn't help but laugh at that thought.

"I'm glad you're okay and your dad too."

"He kind of told a lie about what had happened, but he shared the whole story once I was in front of him. He has meningitis and he had a seizure. He was behind the wheel driving when the accident happened. He didn't want me to know he was in trouble, but talking to him, he's in good spirits. He should be able to go home in a few weeks."

"Do you want to stay with him while he's there?"

"Babe, you're making it seem like you don't need me there. Don't you want Kim to know who I am."

"One thing you should know about me by now is that I'm going to be fine. Of course, we're missing you, we always will, but we will be fine. Your dad needs you. Take your time and be there for him. It's only for a few weeks, right?"

"Yeah, babe, just for a few weeks. No more, maybe less if I can help it."

The first week went by uneventful for Jean and the children. She did miss Tim; he always made her feel like she was the most important person in the world. Jean was getting used to having Kim there. She started experiencing morning sickness, something she hadn't experienced with her previous pregnancies. She hadn't told Tim about the morning sickness, because she knew he would worry.

She kept her word to Tim and Christian by sending pictures of the children every day. She even sent a few videos. Tim thought little Kim was changing right before his eyes. The children were introduced to their grandpa through video. Christian said he couldn't wait to meet them, and he promised he would soon.

The next morning, the doctor said he had some positive news. The swelling had subsided, and the antibiotics were working. If this kept up, they would release him so that he could go home. This pleased Tim and Christian both. Tim called Jean and asked if Christian could hang out with them for a bit. It would be about a month or so before his collarbone finished healing. The doctors were pleased that it was a clean break and didn't leave any fragments.

"Of course, he's welcome here, if that's what you want. Is he okay with that? I'm sure he is used to his independence and all. The children will be very happy to have him here." Tim noticed that Jean sounded excited about the prospect.

"Hey wait, don't get too excited. I haven't asked him about it yet. He may not want to, but I just thought it was an option as long as you were okay with it."

"Babe, he is your dad, like it or not. Whatever it takes for our families to heal, you know I've got your back, front, and side." They both laughed.

"I love you, babe, and I will see you soon."

***

Robert got his wishes. After another week of being in the hospital, his wife was coming home. Mary B and the children had decorated the house for her arrival. Robert had worked hard to make sure the house was wheelchair accessible. He was even proud of the ramp he had built, with William's help of course. Mary B told him that he had become quite handy over the last few years. She also told him that she was proud of him for stepping up and being there for Davina.

"We can't change the past, but we can decide on how we move on from it. You know she loves you, and I know you love her. We often make stupid mistakes when we're young. That's a part of life."

Robert knew he wasn't without fault, and he was glad that Davina and he were working on them. The children were so excited to have her back at home. They loved spending time with her at the hospital, but nothing's better than being at your own home with your own things. The children missed acting out with their mom. Robert missed seeing them interacting with her. Things would be a bit different at least for a while. Robert hoped that being at home would have a positive effect on her. He knew she had the will to walk, but her body just wasn't cooperating.

Davina had been ecstatic when the doctors okayed her going home. She was sick of the hospital food and tired of the smell and the sounds.

"There is no place like home." And she was going there as soon as her husband came to get her. She had already scheduled her physical therapist to come out. Her bags were packed yesterday, Jean had seen to that. Jean was glad she was being released also. She too felt like that would help her with her recovery. Davina's hospital phone rang as soon as Jean walked into the room.

"Hey, Vina Bina, is it okay if Jean comes to get you? I've got a few more things to pick up for the house. I want to make sure we have enough groceries. Is there anything that you need?"

"I need to be at home. That's okay. I will be there soon enough. You go ahead and run your errands. Hopefully, I will be home by the time you get there. I love you." That was the first time she had spoken those words to him, but it felt right. She only hoped he felt the same, even if he didn't vocalize it.

"I love you too, Vina. I will see you soon," he said as he hung the phone up. Davina couldn't resist the smile that came across her face. Jean could only smile too. Things really seemed like they were looking up. Lord knows after what they had all been through. They were due some sunshine.

Over the next few weeks, Davina pushed herself to and beyond her limits. After being home for three weeks, Kaloni and Kevin were playing catch in the house, and the ball accidently hit Davina's leg. She felt the ball as it struck her right leg. It was more of a prick than a pain.

"Kaloni, throw the ball here again, and she pointed to her leg."

"No, Mommy, catch it."

"It's okay, just throw it here."

Kaloni threw the ball to Davina, but when it hit this time, she didn't feel it. Davina let out a sigh of frustration.

Kaloni asked, "Mommy, what's wrong?"

"Nothing's wrong. I was just trying to check something. Thank you, baby, for playing with Mommy."

Davina couldn't wait for Robert to come home to tell him about what had occurred.

"Hey, you won't ever guess what happened a little while ago."

"What, babe? Is everyone okay?"

"Yes, Robert, everyone's okay. I felt something in my leg today."

"What?"

"Nothing bad, I felt some feeling. Well, more of a prick when the children hit me with the ball accidentally. When I tried to recreate the experience, I didn't feel it. I was a little hopeful, but then it was pulled away."

"Babe, you can't get all worked up. We will talk to the doctors and see what they say. Your appointment is next week, right? We'll see what happens over the next few days." Davina tried not to seem disappointed. "It's okay, Davina. We'll get through this. None of that pity party stuff."

Robert was super supportive of Davina, and he was her biggest cheerleader, but he just didn't get it. She felt helpless, no matter how much she pushed herself. She couldn't help but wonder if she was destined to be in that wheelchair for the rest of her life. A part of her felt like it was karma. Another part just felt like she was served an injustice. She was having nightmares, reliving that day she was hit, and her life changed dramatically. Davina hadn't told Robert of the most recent ones. He had no idea she had almost taken her own life several times since she was back at home. If he knew this, he might not be so forgiving. Davina knew she had to seek help, so she decided to confide in Jean. She knew Jean had been through her own set of issues and had demons she still often battled secretly. Davina thought that if anyone would understand her and not judge her, it would be Jean.

***

Christian was excited to be getting released from the hospital. He had already purchased his ticket for his flight home. Although he was grateful to have his son by his side, even if he was acting like a mother hen. Tim had already had his ticket taken care of by his wife. She had gotten him an open-ended ticket; she was smart enough to think ahead. Christian was tired of the Mexican food; he longed for some Down-South fried chicken. Tim had already asked Mary B if she would cook a dinner for their arrival home. Mary B was patiently waiting to meet Tim and Kevin's father. She only knew part of the story, so she was eager to hear the whole thing. Mary B was putting together a grown-up dinner, so they could make sure they were all on one accord.

Tim had missed his family these last three weeks. Even though Jean and he talked everyday several times a day, it wasn't the same. He felt like he had missed out on time with the kids.

Jean had to admit she was ready for her husband to come back. She had been going nonstop. She was about four months and starting to show, and Kim was having some colic issues. Therefore, Jean wasn't getting much rest. She was grateful that Miles and Dayshaun were in school during the day. Mary B had been at the house most days to help her out. But even she was balancing time between there and Robert's house to help Davina out while Robert was at work.

Mary B was happy that her family was getting along well. She couldn't wait to meet Christian. Tim and his father were due to arrive home in time for dinner. Jean was on her way to the airport to meet them. William asked Mary B to take it easy on Tim's father. He didn't commit the act by himself. He also reminded her that everyone seemed to be moving on from it for not only their sake but for the children who were involved. Mary B agreed and told him she was just playing the tough old lady. It really didn't matter what she had to say, but she did want them to enjoy meals together and be a true family. She smiled to herself and thought this was too much for one family. Then she remembered that God doesn't give you more than you can handle.

Jean arrived at the airport just as their flight was landing. She had little Miss Kim in her arms, as always. Kim wasn't ready to be with anyone else except her mom, that is until she saw Tim walking toward her. She had the biggest smile on her face. Tim couldn't help but smile also. He thought it was cute that she seemed to have recognized him. The video calls seemed to have done the trick. Christian walked up and hugged Jean, and kissed Kim on the forehead. Tim grabbed their luggage, and they were ready to go. Jean tried to warn Christian that Mary B could be a handful so just be ready.

"I'm sure that she will eventually love me. If I can win my son back, your momma should be a piece of cake." Tim and Jean both laughed at that.

"You don't know my mom very well."

When they got into the car, Tim sat in the back with Kim, and he played with her the whole ride home. Jean thought to herself, Now I can get some rest.

At that moment, Jean remembered blinking and hearing a crash. She looked over and Christian was okay.

"Tim, Tim, are you okay?"

"Yeah, babe, what a way to be welcomed home. We're okay back here. How about you?"

"I'm okay. I'm so sorry." Jean got out of the car to check the damage. The man in the car behind them also stepped out of his car. He explained that he was just getting in from overseas, and he was in the military. After Tim stepped out and looked at the damage to their back fender, they just decided to exchange information, since it wasn't much damage.

Looking at the piece of paper that he had written his name on, Jean looked back up at him. Tim noticed that Jean seemed a bit on edge, so he tried to speed up the exchange. Once they get back into the car, Jean said to Tim, "You know who that is, don't you? His name is Lucas. I'm almost certain that is Bianca's Lucas. Kim's biological father."

Tim shook his head as if he couldn't believe it. His mind started to wander. "What if he knew, what if he planned that incident?" Tim knew he was probably reaching, but it just seemed strange. Jean told him she would call Bianca tomorrow just to make sure she knew he was back.

Chapter 9

When they arrived at Mary B's, she read them the riot act. "Why are you all late? Dinner is meant to be served hot, not lukewarm."

Robert and Davina had only arrived a few moments before. Formal introductions were made. Jean told her mom about the fender bender, and in the same breath, told her not to worry. Once everyone calmed down and washed their hands, they sat down to eat.

This was as good a time as any to tell Mary B the whole story about Bianca and the story behind Christian. Mary B and William listened in silence as her children shared their stories, occasionally nodding their heads in agreement. She loved the fact that her children had managed again to work out their problems like adults. If nothing else was clear to Christian at the end of the dinner, he knew this family would always be there for each other. He was glad that Tim was a part of such a family.

As far as Kevin, he assured Davina and Robert that he wouldn't interfere. He just wanted them to promise him that he could be a part of his life. He just didn't want him growing up thinking his father didn't want him. Christian also promised that when and if the need arose, he would help financially and physically. Robert told him, they were good financially. His only concern was if Kevin were to get sick. Christian assured him, there were no worries in that area.

Christian's heart went out to Davina when he saw her that night at dinner. Tim had told him what had happened, but he didn't know just how serious it was. That night at dinner, he apologized for pushing her to own up to the truth. He had only done it out of concern and love. Davina told him that it wasn't his fault and she was thankful that he was the man he was. By the end of the night, everyone hugged and shook hands and it felt like family.

Over the next few months, the family had a lot of healing to do, not only physically but mentally as well. Christian's collarbone had healed up nicely, and they had cleared up the meningitis. Robert had remained clean and he had vowed to not use any drugs ever again. He and Davina were talking about renewing their vows. So much had happened, and they thought it might be needed. Davina had been feeling some tingling in her leg but this time she kept quiet about it. She told Robert she wanted to speak to the doctor alone on their last visit.

When she was alone with the doctor, she told him she had been experiencing some tingling in her leg. The doctor asked how long this had been going on, and she told him since a few months. She told him about the first time she felt something when she was playing with the kids, and each time after that. The doctor asked if she had time to run a few tests. Davina nodded. One of the tests the doctor did was test her reflexes, and she didn't understand why he would do that. To her surprise, when he tapped her right knee, there was movement. Tears streamed down her face.

"Don't get too excited just yet. Let me try the other test first." An hour and a half later, after the last test, the doctor called Robert back to the examination room. "First of all, this is what we all hoped for. Your nerves are getting feeling back in them. I'd like to do a procedure that would make a few adjustments to your nerves and tendons. I think we can enhance the feeling in them, and that will allow you to walk sooner than later."

Robert looked at Davina with a smile on his face. She looked back at him with so much hope in her eyes.

"Let's do it," they said in unison.

Davina had an appointment set up for the next week. She was assured that she would only be in the hospital for a few days, and then home with extensive physical therapy. And if they were lucky, she would be able to walk down the aisle when she and Robert renewed their vows. She was excited about being a mother again to her children, as well as a wife to her husband. Robert had been patient, but she knew her husband all too well. One of the things they hadn't discussed was the fact she couldn't give him anymore children. Although Robert said he was okay, she knew he had originally wanted more. Robert was determined to stand by his wife's side, and he did.

Robert and Davina opted not to tell the family about the new developments, in case it didn't work in her favor. She didn't want them feeling sorry for her any more than they already did. Mary B was going to watch the twins while she and Robert went on a small vacation. The procedure wasn't going to be done at the hospital so that lessened the chances of running into Tim, Christian, or Jean.

The surgery was a complete success. The doctor was very optimistic and looked forward to Davina making a full recovery. He instructed Davina to rest for now; she would have to put in some work over the next few weeks. Davina smiled and told him "I'm ready, I've been ready."

And ready she was. Davina began working with the therapist before she left the facility. The therapist had been through something similar, and had to fight her way back as well. Janet had been in a car accident and had been pinned between two cars. She was paralyzed for two years and needed multiple surgeries, and was pushed harder than she had ever been in her life. In the end, it was all worth it. Now she was here to push Davina and show her that she would recover.

Upon her departure from the facility, Janet made arrangements to see her five days a week. She told her to make sure she was ready. There would be no pity party going on. As she left, she saw Robert coming in. Janet remembered Robert from school, but she knew he didn't remember her.

She used to be head over heels in love with him, but he never even noticed her. Janet thought it was ironic that now she was the one assigned to help his wife. She smiled to herself as she admitted that he still looked the same, only a little older. Janet snapped herself out of it and focused on the task at hand. She would do her job and that was it, at least that was what she promised herself. Keeping promises had never been her best quality, but she was determined to stick to this one.

After getting Davina settled in at home, Robert went by his mom's house. He wanted to let them know what was going on with his wife. Mary B was excited, but she promised Robert she would keep quiet about it until Davina had made some progress and wanted everyone to know.

"She has a physical therapist that's coming out five times a week. I think her name is Janet. She mentioned that we went to high school together."

William spoke up, "I seem to remember a young girl named Janet that went to our church around the time you were in high school. I think she had grey eyes and sandy-brown hair."

"I'm not sure if that is the one or not, Pop. I'm sure if you're over the house, you may run into her. She seems nice enough. Davina appears to be happy with her so far. That's the important thing. She may be able to motivate her enough to ensure her progress. She has been through something similar, but she came back from it. She was in a terrible accident, pinned between two cars. For two years, she couldn't walk. But now, she's doing great and helping others."

William resisted the urge to ask his son more questions about Janet. He knew Mary B's mind would start working soon enough. He didn't want to make it any worse.

William's curiosity had been aroused. He needed to see for himself if that was the same little Janet he remembered. It had been awhile since he had seen her. He often wondered what happened to her. Before Mary B came into his life, William had been with Phyllis, who had a little girl around the time she and William broke up. Now Mary B didn't know too much about Phyllis, or Janet for that matter. She had never met them. She knew William had been in a relationship, and that there was a child involved. William had always stood by the fact the child wasn't his. Mary B asked him about it on two separate occasions, and the answer was no both times. That was good enough for her. She trusted William with her life. Everyone had a skeleton or two in their closets. Mary B always knew he was a stand-up type of guy. That was one of the reasons she was attracted to him. Her only condition was that William didn't make her look like a fool if it turned out the child was his. He assured her she had nothing to worry about.

William, for the first few years of her life, had helped Phyllis out financially when it came to Janet. Nothing major, but little odds and ends. In the back of his mind, he always wondered about Janet, but Phyllis had assured him she wasn't his. When she attended the church, he kept an eye on her, but then without notice, she was gone. He knew Phyllis had married and had another child. William hadn't been ready for marriage. He told Phyllis that his grandmother had given him a ring that her father had made himself, he was a blacksmith. William swore that the woman who would wear that ring would be with him forever, and he knew that Phyllis wasn't the one. She had already stepped out on him a few times. William was never really the partying type, except when he was with his friends. So, when she wanted to hang out and have a good time she would often make bad choices. As he suspected one of those bad decisions had resulted in Janet. William made it his business to make sure he went to check on Davina. He couldn't stand not knowing if that was her. He was sure she wouldn't remember who he was and that was just fine. He felt he owed it to himself to make sure she was okay.

Chapter 10

It felt like Mary B needed William's help around the house more than normal. It made him wonder if she was listening when he was talking to Robert the other day. This made William laugh to himself. That was the story of his life. Anytime he was tempted to do something outside of his normal, his wife always seemed to be right there to keep him on the straight and narrow.

William hadn't always been a Christian, or a God-fearing man. When he met Mary B, he used to indulge in drinking and the smoking of cigars. It wasn't long before Mary B put a stop to that. He loved her so much, there wasn't anything he wouldn't do for her to make her happy. It had been that way since the beginning, some things never change.

William had offered to go over to Davina and Robert's to take her some of the homemade soup Mary B had made. She insisted she go with him. It would be good to see the babies; it had been two days she had. He knew when he was beat, so he didn't fight it.

"Come on, woman. Let's get over there so we can get back before it gets too dark. You know my eyesight isn't the best at night."

Yes, Lord, Mary B knew all too well about his eyesight. She had to hear about if for the last few years. She still loved that man, no matter how much he moaned and groaned. Although Mary B played it off, William had no idea she knew he was thinking about that young lady. William had a kind heart and only wanted the best for everyone who he encountered. Mary B had to admit this interest did make her wonder if this young lady was an offspring of her husband. There were some similarities, Robert and Jean both had grey eyes and brown hair. Neither of which William had. She shook it off for now.

Janet was at Davina's house five times a week for at least three hours a day. She didn't want to over work her, but she did want to get an optimal workout from her while she was motivated. Davina and Janet had become very good friends over the last few weeks, and Janet liked that because she didn't have many of those. She had always been an outsider. Even when she was a child she was taunted because she didn't know who her father was. Her mom always told her that he was just a guy that she slept with once and he wasn't around afterwards. It used to bother her when she was growing up, but now she was over it. She was done feeling sorry for herself. One of her attractions for Robert was his grey eyes. She would daydream about what their children would look like. Now many years later that thought still was on her mind. Robert made it hard for her to just stay focused on helping his wife. She had caught glimpses of him after he was done showering. He was tempting her, and he didn't even know it. As each day went by, she was valuing her friendship with Davina more and more. She remembered the promise she made to herself and she dug her heels in and intended to stand her ground.

Just as Janet was about to leave for the day, Mary B and William arrived. After introductions were made of course Mary B and William both had all sorts of questions for this young lady.

"How are you doing, Janet? We're so grateful for you and what you're doing for Davina."

"Oh no, she's helping me. She's making me look really good. She has been making some progress. I hope we will have something to show you all real soon."

Mary B couldn't wait any longer, enough of the small talk. "So where are you from?"

"I'm actually from right here. My mom and I lived here for many years. She got married and had another child, and we moved until my high school days. Then we returned."

"What does your mom do, if I may ask? I'm sorry. I know it seems like I'm bombarding you with questions."

"It's okay. I don't mind the questions. I guess you want to be sure who is around your family. I think I would be the same way if I had family like that. My mom was a seamstress. She passed some years ago.

My stepfather was a jerk, so he and my little brother moved back to Africa. He said American women were not accommodating. He tried to control me, and I wasn't having it so he paid for my tuition for school and kept money in my account and I've not seen him for several years now. I went to school with your children. I was shy and kind of an outcast back then, so they probably never really noticed me." Just then Robert came in the room, "Mom dad are you grilling her, she may never come back." "Not a chance of that Robert, Davina and I got a lot vested in her making a full recovery. For now, you guys are stuck with me."

There was something vaguely familiar about this young lady. There was something in those eyes of hers. She knew she had seen them somewhere and it wasn't in William. Mary B wouldn't rest until she figured it out, that's for sure.

William looked at Janet as Mary B was asking her one thousand and one questions, and he knew that was the Janet he remembered, except now she was all grown up. From the sounds of it, her life hadn't been the one he would have chosen for her. He was happy that she was okay. That was his main concern. He couldn't help but look from Robert to Janet and back again, he was looking for signs that they came from the same genes. He couldn't see any resemblance except for the eye color and the hair. That wasn't enough to upset the balance of his family. Things had finally started settling down. Still, William had to be sure. The wheels in his brain started turning. He knew he wouldn't be able to let it rest.

Janet having been held up long enough; she excused herself and told them she would see them next time. She had called and ordered take out and really needed to get going. William helped her with her jacket, and when doing so he noticed a few strands of her hair were on the collar. He brushed them into his hand and said his goodbyes, so he could throw them in the trash. Only they never made it. He made his way to the kitchen and put them inside of a sandwich bag. He had been swift no one noticed what had happened not even Mary B's watchful eyes. William went into the bathroom where he knew he would find some strands in Robert's brush. He grabbed a few of those and put them into the other bag he had in his jacket pocket. Now he just had to figure out the rest of his plan.

Christian had been enjoying his time with his grandchildren. His collarbone was finally healed, and his son was happy. He had even reached out and started getting to know Jeff who was now married with a son of his own. Christian advised him to make sure they check him to make sure he wasn't at risk of kidney disease. Jeff assured him that he would make sure they took care of it. Now that he was all healed up, there was no reason for him to continue staying and being a burden to Tim and Jean. He admitted to himself that he wasn't really looking forward to leaving but he knew it was going to happen eventually. He was due to go back to work in a few weeks, so he had a little time, before he had to bring it up. Things were going well, with Davina and Robert, and he was able to see Kevin regularly. He didn't envy Davina when it came time to tell them if it ever did, that they shared their mom but had different dads. He knew that wouldn't be easy. Christian and William had become close over the last few weeks. That was something that Christian wasn't used too. He had his colleagues in the medical field but no one to just hang out with and watch the games or go to a live game. He learned that William liked basketball, almost as much as he liked hockey. He used to play in college. The guys had gone out to a few games and to play pool a few times. They called it their boys night out. It drove the women crazy because they would come home and act like they had been drinking and hitting on all the ladies. The women would always pretend that they were upset and call each other; it was the game they played.

Robert was feeling encouraged with Davina and her progress, she was determined. He loved seeing her passion for walking again. She had lost hope on more than one occasion that was something he didn't want to see often. They had been through a lot and overcame it. He was thankful that they fought their way through and back to each other. Their house had never been happier. The only concern that he could honestly say he had was when he caught Janet starring at him a few times too many. He didn't say anything to Davina about it because she was working hard, and he didn't want to disrupt that. He told himself he would keep an eye on it to see if it continued.

Don't forget to sign up for

Mind Flow Publishing & Production LLC's Newsletter @

www.mindflowpublishingproduction.com

Email us for autographed or additional paperback copies @

mindflowpubpro@gmail.com

$3.95 is added for shipping & handling

Other Titles Also Available Include

Mental Interlude – Poetry

The Mary B Chronicles – Fiction

Journey to Living (kindle only) – Inspirational

Simple Complexity – Poetry

Available Through

Amazon

Barnes & Noble

Kindle

Coming Soon

The Mary B Chronicles Book III – Fiction

The Mary B Chronicles Book IV -- Fiction

Charisma's Homecoming -- Fiction

Dreams Do Come True – Fiction

Upcoming Titles Will Be Available Through

Amazon

Barnes & Noble

Kindle

Apple ibooks

Kobo

P.S. Don't forget to leave a review @ amazon, goodreads, barnes&nobles

www.ingramcontent.com/pod-product-compliance
Ingram Content Group UK Ltd.
Pitfield, Milton Keynes, MK11 3LW, UK
UKHW022237230426
12048UKWH00018BA/1313